The Misstep of Heather Bainbridge

By

C.D. Faulconer

Deep Indigo Books
Published by Indigo Sea Press
Winston-Salem

Deep Indigo Books
Indigo Sea Press
302 Ricks Drive
Winston-Salem, NC 27103

This book is a work of fiction. Names, characters, locations and events are either a product of the author's imagination, fictitious or used fictitiously. Any resemblance to any event, locale or person, living or dead, is purely coincidental.

Copyright 2015 by C.D. Faulconer

First Deep Indigo Books edition published
March, 2016
Deep Indigo Books, Moon Sailor and all production design are trademarks of Indigo Sea Press, used under license.

For information regarding bulk purchases of this book, digital purchase and special discounts, please contact the publisher at
indigoseapress.com

Cover design by Stacy Castanedo

Manufactured in the United States of America
ISBN 978-1-63066-393-3

Dedication

In memory of my husband, Tom, who spoke in soft demands to fill these pages; who owned my heart and was my second Reason.

I also dedicate this to my sister-in-law and dear friend, Marie Jilek, because when the rain beat cold and shivering, she brought turquoise waters and bent the tea leaves in my soul toward God.

Psalm 65

(The Fides Translation)

For you have tested us, O God,

You have tried us with fire, as silver is tried:

You have led us into a snare,

laid a great burden on our backs:

You have let men ride us down,

we have gone through fire and water,

then You led us out to freedom.

PART ONE

Chapter One

"Am I going to lose everything? All happiness?" Claire wondered, and knew she would forever remember this day as one of those few major events in a lifetime that stand above all others.

The year was 1950. It was a Tuesday. The California autumn was warm and mild. There were no clouds, only the blue illumined sky. From the trees, birds sang forth like glee clubs as her sister, Jeanette, strapped three-month-old, red-headed Heather, into the small portable container attached in the rear seat of her station wagon. When a family moves, there isn't much room, so Claire helped by pushing every which way in order not to waste even an inch of space inside her sister's car.

What she had been fighting all morning, the aching swelling sadness, began to crawl up her throat and crowd her thinking as the packing neared completion. Her sister, Jeanette, and brother-in-law, Mark, with their baby, Heather, would be living far away. Mark had been chanting, "Nevada, Nevada, that's where we're a-viting to," all morning like an unwelcome promise. When he wasn't singing it, he was whistling the same silly tune. If there was sorrow in his tall lean frame of a body, atop which sat a square face, light blue eyes, and red curly hair, Claire couldn't detect it. "More for less," had been Mark's conclusion to every financial discussion for three years, usually with a follow-up that ran, "California is for deep pockets, and I have none of those. Someday, we're heading where door-stops are gold and champagne flows like the Nile."

Mark and Jeanette had decided on a tiny town called Sage, in the middle of Nevada, where the nearest doctor was 100 miles away down a ribbon of a road cut through the desert as though a giant had dragged a stick behind himself while emptying his pockets of shimmering dust. Mark bought out the retiring hardware store owner and the store's limited stock of items. It didn't matter that it was a stark beginning, Mark acted as though he had been crowned King of the World.

Their Nevada house had three bedrooms, two bathrooms, a front and back yard, and was clustered with 200 other souls embedded in this village at the desolate heart of the state. There was even a small swimming pool off the rear deck from the master bedroom. The real estate agent said the only other pool in town was a community facility used in summer, mainly by children, because the adults were too busy scratching together the basics of life. Along with the doctor, the convenience stores were also 100 miles away, down that same mirage path radiating its white heat and interrupting the barren landscape as it stretched into the horizon as far as the eye could see.

Claire smiled wanly at the embarrassed glances Jeanette occasionally gave her this morning. It would be their first separation, and already Claire dreaded not being able to pick up the telephone to talk with her sister or stop by for an afternoon cup of coffee and to cuddle little Heather.

"All aboard!" Mark quipped, then hugged Claire, finishing his embrace by kissing her forehead with a loud smack. "Off to the frontier," he proclaimed, sliding behind the driver's wheel, followed by his chanting melody of, "More for less, we're off to where there's more for less. All aboard!"

He turned and tickled Heather on her neck causing her to smile and scrunch up in pink pleasure.

Jeanette came to face Claire, her eyes filled with tears. Her mouth moved, but silently. Claire reached for her sister and pulled her to herself for a long oneness that needed no words. When they opened their embrace, Jeanette closed her eyes, nodded her head up and down, then turned quickly and entered the front passenger side of the car.

Atop the tall white daisies, butterflies begin and end. They repeat yellow, purple, and white, as they live through perils and gladness in their lifetime of one day; and it is enough.

Like a melting, the square white vehicle, with its extra

carrying pod atop, and the only three people in the universe Claire could call "family" pulled away, becoming smaller and smaller until her loved ones were a speck in the distance. Then they were gone. Claire stared at the spot where they had disappeared and felt like part of her body had been ripped off. After several numb moments she forced herself into motion and walked slowly back to her car.

It was exactly 3:06 a.m. when the phone atop Claire's bed-stand rang. It wasn't yet twenty-four hours since her family had gone. A call at this hour felt like a bullet already discharged, singing through time and space with its song of death.

In a frightened stampede, Claire's thoughts ran from her. She stared at the phone's ringing and felt her heart begin to race. Maybe someone drank too much and dialed a wrong number that came as this red light into her sleep. Yes, that must be what happened she decided, and watched her hand reach slowly for the telephone. She lifted the receiver to her ear, and waited. There was silence on the other end of the phone line. Without understanding why, Claire felt a womb of time exploding without sound around her, birthing a floating surrealism.

"Hello?" came a man's voice from the receiver. "Is this the residence of Claire Summers?"

Somehow, through her clutching throat, Claire answered, "Who is calling?"

"I'm Sherriff Meadows, Ma'am, from Sage, Nevada. I'm sorry to call you at this late hour, but I need to know if you are the sister of Jeanette Bainbridge."

It was a distant voice, separate from her, that somehow squeezed from the high corner of her bedroom wall and answered for her, "Jeanette? Nevada?"

"Yes, Ma'm. Are you the sister of Jeanette Bainbridge?"

An image of her beloved sister flew in front of her sight. "Yes," she answered, barely audible.

"I'm sorry to say I have bad news, Ma'am. There's been an accident."

"Accident?" Claire repeated like a robot.

The man cleared his throat. "I regret to inform you that your sister and her husband have been killed in an automobile accident."

3

Stones cry out, the moon screams, mutes blare, because Claire's silence was greater than these. She was a siren of absent sound.

"Mrs. Summers?"

The summons confused her. "What? What did you say?"

"I'm sorry, Ma'am."

Claire forced herself to focus. She had to know all of it. She could barely make her voice work. "The baby?" she squeaked.

"Beg your pardon, Ma'am?"

Hoarsely, Claire repeated, "What about the baby? Heather? Is she..."

"No, Ma'am. She's fine. Not even a scratch. Sometimes you see that in my line of work. A whole vehicle will be smashed flat except for one little pocket around someone that holds steady and doesn't buckle at all. It's a miracle."

"Where is she? Where is Heather?"

"We're a small town, Ma'am. Our pastor's wife is caring for her. She's a nurse. Meanwhile, I'm doing the required paperwork and notifying the next of kin."

"I'll leave this morning. I'll come by plane."

"I'm sorry, Ma'am, but we don't have an airport. The nearest one is 100 miles from here."

Think, Claire, think. "Do you have any flat land nearby?"

"Yes, Ma'am. The surrounding area is entirely flat."

"Somehow, I'll land there. Somehow...somehow..." her voice trailed off.

"Yes, Ma'am."

"And Sheriff Meadows?"

"Yes, Ma'am?"

"... Never mind. I'll be there today."

"Good night, Ma'am."

Her mouth moved silently in a "good-night" shape, as the phone slid from her ear and fumbled back into its cradle.

Claire's thoughts ricocheted.

I see the haunting and hear chains rattle along absent steps. Where is my war-horse? Where is Heaven? In the corner box are letters and dead spiders and skeletons from when life was fat.

The Misstep of Heather Bainbridge

Deer Antie Claire.

My teecher sed wee cood tri sending this pin cooshun to mommie in heven for muthers day. I mayd it pink beecuz pink is a girl coler. Do you thenk we shuld send needels and thred two? My frend, Betti, hlped me spel, even tho I am a first graydr and she is a secon graydr.

Love, Heather
p.s. if it dus not reech momma, I want you to hav it.

She was proxy. She was in the world making arrangements for a small plane to fly her to Sage, Nevada. She could see herself working over the details but she wasn't there. She was drowning and no one could breathe her water.

The pilot she hired assisted her into the aircraft and within minutes the ground had dropped away as they climbed into a clear blue morning, a morning that felt like death was a lie.

Say it isn't true. Dive into my heart. Be springtime and ten thousand yellow daffodils covering hillsides. Turn cheerful this horror in my soul.

"It's a good day to fly over the mountains," the pilot shared, "otherwise, that Sierra Range down there can be devilish to get over."

The man's voice broke Claire's numbness. Looking out the plane's small window, she focused on the pine trees below, many laden with snow. There were large stretches of granite; some smooth, or twisted, or laddered like a series of petrified waves. Snow lay in deep pockets where the gray surfaces slumped. Such a vast ancient expression of earth's tonnage as magma fires of unimaginable violence had cooled in these wild natural ways eons ago. Even in her anguish, Claire appreciated the raw beauty of what she saw.

She noticed mountain roads and how they often followed the edge of some dizzying precipice. Occasionally, here, high above the valleys, an otherwise hidden lake flashed the Sun's reflection like a Morse code of interstellar language.

Nonetheless, all this beauty could not efface the awful

destination Claire both longed and dreaded to reach. How could she only yesterday have felt the loving person of her younger and only sister in her arms, and now that sister be gone forever? In ghostly mockery, the last chirpings of her brother-in-law, Mark, came back to her like death blows. "More for less, more for less."

The pilot landed in a small dirt field behind one of the two small rows of buildings lining what Claire assumed was the main street of this tiny rustic settlement. An old dented blue truck drove towards them before the plane's propellers had come to a full stop. A short man, probably in his 60's, climbed from the truck. Claire noticed the man's thick heavy hair with its former blond color showing through the gray.

"Claire Summers?" he asked, extending his hand. "I'm Sheriff Meadows."

Claire nodded as they shook hands, noticing he was a pale man, and seemed to have a gentle demeanor. "I wish you were arriving in Sage for different reasons, Mrs. Summers. We're all sorry about the accident and what's happened to your family."

Claire was confused by his expression, "we're all," assuming he meant the police force. "How many officers do you have in Sage?" she asked, desperate to keep a semblance of normalcy in her thinking and conversation, while at the same time terrifying emotions swelled and cataracted into her deepening hole of loss. Her footing stumbled, and her mouth was dry. She heard words coming out of the mouth of Sheriff Meadows but she understood only a portion of what he was saying. In a dark chamber and behind the red curtain at the center of her heart, she sat curled and staring. On the surface she heard her voice, but felt detached, as though she was watching an actor playing her part.

"Oh, I don't mean police, Ma'am, I'm the only one of those. We're a little over 200 people in Sage so when something happens everybody knows about it. We're isolated and we stick together."

He helped her into his truck as the pilot announced he would go his way until the following morning. The moment the truck's engine started Claire's first question came quickly. "How did it happen?"

Marry lightning and sand so I can hold onto something. I'm falling. Help me keep the ledge.

"A storm, Ma'am. We get big ones, and quick, out here. Until you get used to them they can be real dangerous. It was thirty miles down the highway, about halfway through Big Smoky Valley. The road is a two-laner and straight as a ruler as far as the eye can see. The traffic was light but the wind was blowing hard and rain was coming down sideways and heavy. The driver of the truck said your brother-in-law swerved into him like he had lost control of the car. There was nothing the Trucker could do to avoid it. The skid marks proves his story is true. There's a hundred feet of brake rubber that never leaves the Trucker's lane. Your brother-in-law's car left skid marks that zigzagged then swept in a half circle right into the path of the truck. I'm afraid the vehicle folded up like a bellows, Ma'am." He stopped and glanced at Claire. "If it's any consolation to you, it was quick. They didn't know what hit them." Sheriff Meadows cleared his throat, then offered, "Perhaps there's mercy in that."

"Mercy?" Claire thought. She hadn't considered mercy, even though she believed in mercy. She also believed life was an unpredictable crosshair.

For now, her soul was too overwrought with sorrow and had no room for the inevitable 'Why?' and its guessing answers.

"My sister and brother-in-law? Are their bodies? I mean, are they..."

"Yes, they're recognizable. I'm sorry you have to go through this, but you're the next of kin and it's the law."

Dear Aunty Claire,

Happy Mothers Day. I like second grade. Today Miss Little our teecher pushed the wrong buton on our movie prajektor and the swimer came out bakward from the swiming pool. He looked silly with feet cumming out of the water then landing bak on the dyving bord. It was fun. See you after skool.

Love, Heather
second grade

Sheriff Meadows took Claire to a small rock building that

appeared handmade. Claire knew this area was rich in minerals and guessed the building-blocks were quarried locally. They were a type of Shale or Sandstone mortared together to form four walls, atop which sat a corrugated metal roof, that at a glance admitted to have been used on other roofs in former days. Claire focused on the quarried material, admiring the intrinsic beauty of red streaking through the yellow stone. She knew she was trying anyway she could to steel herself for what lay ahead. The finality of death filled and sickened her senses.

"We don't have an official Coroner's office, Mrs. Summers," Sheriff Meadows offered, as he led Claire past the tiny front desk area, paneled in what she recognized as Pinion pine. She followed reluctantly as they issued through another opening into a larger room, poorly lit, with boxes and a feeling of storage to it. The overall atmosphere was a sensation of dust and cobwebs.

Against the back wall Claire made out four flat-topped tables. Two of them were occupied. Coarse brown woolen blankets lay over what were obviously two stilled bodies.

The arrow slices the apple of the eye. The arrow is welcome because it blinds. Let go of the bowstring so the arrow can rescue me.

Claire froze, unable to take another step. The hours since the phone call from Sheriff Meadows, the flight to Sage, all this time she had suppressed the shock, had held it back by sheer willpower. She was hasty concrete in the Monsoon, forcing her thoughts to think about her work with shut-ins, or the arrangements needed to get a bedridden widow to her doctor. It was fear and denial. It was hazy nihilism, but Claire had always despised turning one's back on reality with its never-ending hardships.

Sheriff Meadows offered, "I wish I could give you some of my experience. There's kind of a protective shell you eventually grow." He shrugged his shoulders, then admitted, "This is the worst part of my job. May we take a look?"

Claire nodded 'yes'.

"You stand here. You don't have to view the body, only the face. All we need is a quick look to get a positive identification." He was quiet for a moment, then added, "But of course, you take as long as you want."

Sheriff Meadows lifted the corner of one blanket, uncovering Mark's face. Claire heard the sudden intake of breath fill the room with sound, vaguely realizing it had come from her. Quickly, Sheriff Meadows covered the face again. "Is this your brother-in-law, Mark Bainbridge?"

Claire squeezed her eyes shut, swallowed hard, then shook her head up and down violently.

It is tattooed. The ink will never fade. My mind knows forever what it just saw.

Turning, Sheriff Meadows pulled the cloth from off the face of the second body.

Claire was staring blindly at the ceiling.

"Please, Ma'am. I'm sorry. Only just take a moment so we can be absolutely certain."

She forced her eyes to look. Jeanette! My sweet baby sister, Jeanette! Nothingness is mercy. The room disappeared as Claire sank into darkness.

When she revived, she was in a chair back in the office area. Sheriff Meadows and several other people surrounded her. The first person Claire focused on was a round-faced, middle-aged woman, with short dark wavy hair, and honey-colored large-rimmed glasses.

"Hello, Claire," the woman addressed her, "I'm Emily Brown. You might say I'm the local doctor since we don't have a doctor in Sage and I'm a registered nurse. I'm also the pastor's wife. We've been watching Heather until you arrived." She patted Claire's arm. "You rest a few minutes longer then we'll go to my place and see Heather."

Heather! She had forgotten all about Heather! In the ugly necessity of...the thoughts began to suck light into an oblivious hole again, but at that very moment, Claire felt a gentle massaging on her shoulders from Emily who had stepped behind her. It was enough to dispel the darkness. Leaning over, Emily offered softly, "The worst is over. From this time forward you will begin to heal, and having Heather will help you."

Be a moving laugh inside this shocked and shattered body and brain.

Emily's voice had a western drawl to it and resonated sweetly. Claire sensed sincerity and strength at the root of this woman.

Papers were signed and Claire drank two cups of strong black coffee, then said she was ready to see Heather. The people in the office were in motion all at once. Claire had the impression this town was one body and when one part moved, so moved the whole.

Two worlds were within her. She felt like iron, weighed down with blows that sparked and burned; and at the same time there was ether whispering laments into her soul like a visit from the dead. She rose up and followed silently behind Emily.

Chapter Two

These runnels, they flow to the sea and become understanding.

Dear Auntie Claire,

Third grade is cool. David dosn't bother me now becuz he likes Sue. Thank you for being my mother. Happy Mother's Day.
All my love,
Heather

In a rocking chair, snuggled in the arms of a teenage girl feeding her with a bottle, a baby's attention was fixed on the young face above her. In an instant, Claire recognized the soft curly red hair of her niece. Moving into view above the teenager Claire stooped down, speaking sounds of love and greeting. Heather stopped her noisy pulling upon the nipple of the bottle, then smiled and cooed at her aunt. "May I?" Claire asked, then sat down and gathered Heather to herself. She reapplied the bottle to her tiny sucking mouth. Rocking, she repeated, "I love you, little Heather, I love you."

Here the knot is tight even if the ends fly away. This spot concentrates like a petrifying.

Claire rocked while Heather gurgled happily between swallows, blinking each time tears from above landed against her pink cheeks.

A dozen folks helped at the airplane, all of them focusing on Claire and Heather.

"I'll have your sister and brother-in-laws' remains shipped to *Chamberlain Funeral Home* in Walnut Glen," Sheriff Meadows told her quietly aside. "You can expect them to arrive within a week." Nervously clearing his throat, he added, "We prayed for you and the baby this morning in church."

11

C.D. Faulconer

Incense rises to Heaven.

"Good luck, Ma'am," he offered, helping her into the passenger side of the small aircraft along with a dozen other helping hands.

Emily handed Claire a large cloth bag with straps. "The ladies at church put this together for you. It will help until you can get to the store for baby items." Emily lifted the bundle containing Heather up to her. "God Bless!" she finished, backing away from the plane as its propellers swirled into a blur.

Beginning their taxi across the field, a dense plume of dust rose behind them. Claire turned and saw the townspeople jumping into their vehicles to escape the cloud. Only two figures remained fixed; Sheriff Meadows and Emily.

Circling, then gaining altitude, Claire saw the cluster of Sage citizens below, now out of their vehicles, waving and watching the airplane's progress through the sky. Here, in quiet obscure Sage, somewhere in the middle of a big empty desert state, where life seemed inviolable and detached from earth itself, Claire had found a group of no-nonsense people who loved their church, one another, and those in need even from outside their town limits.

The pilot was quiet on their return flight and politely excused himself when they were landed back at Walnut Glen's airport and he had escorted Claire and Heather to Claire's blue station wagon. Her car was parked indifferently at the edge of the parking lot, only dustier, Claire noticed.

It seemed impossible that she was holding Heather under these circumstances. Her long-awaited niece had finally been born to a thirty-seven-year-old mother. How many times Claire and Jeanette had marveled that as soon as Jeanette had given up on ever having a baby, she became pregnant.And now, Claire, at forty-years-old, would raise that baby.

She decided that nothing mattered more than to have Jeanette and Marks' child raised under her personal love and care. She would do this because she loved Heather, and because Jeanette still lived through this baby.

Dear Auntie Claire,

12

Happy Mother's Day. 4th grade is fun excep for the boys. They act stupid. My teacher, Mrs. McDonald, says I am good with reading but not so great at math. She is helping me with that. Thank you for helpingme at home with it too. And for being such a wondurful mother.

Love, Heather

"How is your niece?" Claire's friend asked.

Claire leaned over and fluffed the pillows of the invalid.

"She is a blossoming beauty. She's fair-skinned and has freckles, like her mother. Her build is medium but on the smaller side, and she has the most radiant head of red wavy hair you ever saw. My sister's was more of an auburn color, and Mark's was carrot orange, but Heather's color is in-between.

"Jeanette had a gentle demeanor and I think Heather will take after her mother in that way."

We are spirals that meet and catch as the dance of life continues. We each bring our balls of string to tie together then throw into open chance.

Claire felt a lump in her throat and wondered if she would ever be able to speak of her beloved sister without pain. "Now tell me what's been going on with you since last week. What did your doctor say?"

The frail lady began a detailed description of the pieces and parts of her weaknesses, as Claire sat in a tattered chair alongside the bed listening. For nine years, this bedroom was the only world known to the sick elderly woman Claire visited once a week to convey a sense of the world caring and continuing its stream into the life of this bedridden woman. Often, in the warmer months when the only window in this small bedroom of pale blue walls and scuffed hardwood floors, was opened, Claire was struck by its contrast with outside life, where horns honked, booming music played loudly from passing cars, and voices floated in from people walking along the sidewalk down the gravel road from this neglected old house. It was a neighborhood unaware of this woman's illness and solitary plight bound to a

13

sickbed. New houses had sprouted with deep green grass added in rolls to look as though it had been growing and nurtured for years. Trees were beginning to catch on to life and aspire upward in their new sites where they would trust the years to allow them to flourish. Then this little shambles of a house where Claire now sat, in the middle of all the newness and starting out of lawns and young families and their dreams. All of that was the reverse of disease, which squeezes out that which is old and tired.

Claire felt that this small shabby dwelling was the most felicitous structure of all, because of what it housed, a godly woman overlooked, even forsaken by the world; the spinning, chasing, non-penalty world, where everyone writes their own universe.

Dear Aunt Claire,
Poetry is a blast. My teacher says I am good with words. The boys are better in 5th grade. They dont act stupid and step on the girls shoos any more. Some are even nice. One of the boys, Mike, tells each girl she is the only girl for him. I wonder why he just doesn't pick one and stick to her? This year for Mothers Day I decided to write a longer letter because I am older and know how to write better. I know we talk about mom and dad and that you loved them very much. I wish I coud remember them, but in a way I know them because of all the things you tell me about them. They sound like super peeple. Sometimes the other kids act funny tord me because I'm not like them. I don't have a mom and a dad at home. I feel bad when they do that. They dont get it when I tell them you are my mom and dad. Maybe someday they will undurstand.

I love you like one real mom and one real dad,
Heather

Claire was there when Heather rolled over for the first time. At four months old and delighted with her new found motion, Heather began rolling from the living room into the kitchen until the lower cabinets of red and yellow Cocobolo paneling stopped her progress. When she tried to get past this solid barrier but couldn't, she raised loud scoldings until Claire scooped her up, held her high, and jiggled her little round body causing Heather to squeal with delight. Putting her down, Heather would continue rolling, until once again something blocked the way and her wailing brought Claire to lift her once more, kissing first one cheek and then the other, until Heather's drool fell from an open giggling mouth. This was their first game.

Heather soon learned that the straighter she held her body the faster she could roll. To Claire she looked like a little log with fire at one end. Sometimes she stopped wherever she happened to be and fell asleep, punctuated with cooing, sudden intakes of breath, and occasional jerks of her body. Claire would lay a blanket over her and slip a pillow under her head, thinking, thinking how much she wished Jeanette could be here to see her precious darling child.

The longer Claire played with her, the more Heather's cheeks glowed and her tiny laugh rose, filling the house with irresistible joy.

She learned to smack her hands together and make a clapping noise, or when she was on her back she would swing her legs into the air then try to catch them. When she caught her feet they were her treasure to twist and turn before letting go only to try and catch them again.

Her energy was boundless, but she also needed more sleep than other infants her age. Claire allowed her to take her natural length of sleeping time and never woke her because it was this time or that time or some call of the wild time or the swamping, mundane, demanding, insisting, and at times intrusive grabbing for one's time to suck that energy into the useless. Heather was a sleeper and Claire protected that need.

Once Heather began walking nothing was less than fascinating to her, not even a corner bundle of dust. This beginning of her tactile life charmed Claire, as if she herself was feeling the textures of life again for the first time.

The social atmosphere of Claire's and Heather's home was sometimes busy, as Claire worked to assist those that were forgotten or kicked to one side to starve and die; so severe were the needs of some of her clients.

Heather was over a year old and walking if she could hold onto furniture as she walked. When a large space presented itself where nothing could steady her balance, she resorted to crawling until she reached the next piece of furniture where she got onto her feet again and continued along her way. Often, she would arrive at the knees of one of Claire's clients and shout a sound meant to be a greeting. She bounced on her pudgy legs, and if the client leaned down to her level and baby-talking or stroked her brilliant red hair, Heather's delight knew no bounds. Her squeal was joyous and her large blue eyes invited the whole world to come in.

One sunny morning in the month of August, a stout young man with black hair came for an appointment with Claire, in hopes she could steer him to a possible job. He had been out of work 15 months. His car had been re-possessed and the house was in foreclosure. Claire learned that he lived with his mother and father.

As he sat talking to Claire, Heather came cooing and gurgling and stumbling along the walls from the kitchen and approached the man. When she was directly in front of him, as she had been with so many of Claire's clients, she slapped his knees and giggled. From her one-toothed mouth came drool that caused her chin to shine. Her greeting of the dark-haired man was total in its enthusiasm.

It burst from him, as though kept under too long, a loud dark rejection into Heather's face causing her to stumble backwards and fall. A brief silence passed before Heather let out a terrified scream. It was as though it took time for her young brain to find a place to lodge this mortified memory.

Claire was to Heather in seconds, swiftly picking her from off the ground and clutching her tightly to her breast. Savagely, she turned to the man, who sat still and unconcerned as if nothing was out of the ordinary. "You leave my house this instant and don't ever come here again!"

The man shrugged his shoulders then walked slowly across the room and out the front door, calm as a sunbathing cat.

Heather's body was in a fury, shaking as though ice ran through her veins. Her face was pale except for round hectic spots, red as apples that showed on her cheeks. She remained in this condition the rest of the day and into the night, perspiration causing her soft red hair to stick to her forehead and along the sides of her face.

Anxiously, Claire dabbed Heather's face and neck and body with cool washrags, talking all the while with words Heather could not understand except by their tonal qualities that said, "You are okay. I am here. I love you. You are safe from fear or harm."

As Heather's body cooled and the whimpering turned to an occasional gasp, she finally drifted off to sleep.

We learn that life will not be predicted and vulnerability belongs to every moment. The wish for peace and accordance lies within most breasts, but always, there will be the stalker whose only peace is pain and suffering imposed upon others.

It was several days before the experience effaced from Heather's countenance. She was clinging to Claire more and frequently cried when Claire was out of sight, but gradually her buoyancy returned and she was once again giggling and laughing and even walking tipsy between her short destinations. Claire noted, however, that when clients came to their home, Heather never approached them as she had before.

The shriek of her experience with the dark-haired man had sunk in and made a substance of itself; a substance that would be a tiny uneasy spot inside Heather for the rest of her life.

By the time Heather was three, Claire knew she had followed her mother's soft personality and shyness. Her father, Mark, had been the polar opposite with his big openness and easy ability to insinuate himself into conversations with friends or strangers.

Heather now stayed toward the back or edge when other people were around.

In some rudimentary way, Heather sensed what pleased Claire and would set off on her busy intention to make Claire smile and be happy with her. "Bananas there," she spouted when Claire brought their groceries into the kitchen. Then she would take her yellow load to a wire basket and place the bananas inside. "Oranges here," she chirped, and placed the oranges one-by-one into the fruit drawer of the refrigerator. And on it would go until the bags were empty. Then Claire would gather the top of the thin smaller bags, blow into them until they were bulging, and hold it out toward Heather. Quickly, Heather would hit the bag until it popped, sending her into paroxysms of giggles.

Heather called Claire "Mama," but sometimes used the word, "Papa." Claire wondered if this young child who witnessed and lived through a horrific automobile accident that killed her parents could know, instinctively, or deep in some vague memory without words, that her real parents were gone. Like a runt tossed from an animal litter, could Heather feel thrown away in spite of Claire's adoring love?

Down in the rudiments of consciousness where the floor and walls and roof are built to contain the whole of life's experiences, did the car crash put a rusty nail into the floorboard of Heather's life?

Soon after Heather's 5th birthday, it was a Saturday, Claire and Heather were in the kitchen sprinkling colored crystal sugars over freshly-baked cookies. Claire stepped aside so Heather could be in charge of the decorating. Her pouring was not a well-spaced outcome, but she worked with a sense of fun seriousness.

The doorbell rang and Claire left Heather with her tongue protruding out one corner of her mouth as she concentrated on her sprinkling efforts.

"Hello, Helen, come in."

A large woman with a head not proportioned to the largeness of her body stepped inside. She swept a curly lock of brunette hair from her forehead.

Helen had been Claire's neighbor for 10 years. They were close in age, but Claire had rarely mingled with Helen and her friends, except at the beginning. An avid Bridge player, Helen's love for Bridge and a following tea party had put Claire off because the conversations over the cards and tea had mainly been a bragging race to see who could outdo the others in various arenas of life.

Who was the richest? Who lived in the most expensive neighborhood? Who had the greater square footage? Whose car had the right emblem? Who could lift her chin highest, even without realizing its pedestrian arrogance?

Frankly, it was a huge bore to Claire and soon Helen stopped inviting her after Claire's many polite refusals. Since then, their relationship was cordial and no more, but Claire often paused and talked with Helen's daughter, Patti.

"Claire, I have something to show you," Helen indicated a large bag at her side.

"Let's sit here on the couch, Helen. Would you like a cup of coffee?"

"No, thank you, it makes my teeth chatter after one cup and I had my quota this morning." After sitting and scooting and pushing her brown and white polka-dot dress this way and that and setting her shoulders just so, Helen opened the bag and showed its contents to Claire. Inside was a veritable collection of Heather's possessions, including the new fuzzy pink sweater with pearl-like buttons that Claire had purchased for Heather earlier in the week.

Confused, Claire looked up at Helen. "These are Heather's things. How did you get them?"

"I'm embarrassed to say this, but Patti played cards with Heather for gifts. Of course Patti won every hand because she's five years older than Heather. Each time she won she told Heather to go home and get something nice to give her. She said Heather was happy to do it and after an hour of playing all these items had been handed over to Patti. I'm sorry," Helen finished, offering the bag to Claire, "I've given Patti a severe scolding for taking advantage of Heather. You may want to talk with Heather about it too."

"Sometimes red pitchforks lean against these walls."

"I will talk to her. Thank you for letting me know, Helen."

Standing to leave, a few common amenities were exchanged and Helen walked out the door.

For several minutes, Claire sat over the bag, cataloguing in her mind that all the items inside were Heather's favorite things.

"Did she value them so little? Could she have a desperation to please that was stronger than her love of the things in life she treasured?"

Returning to the kitchen, Claire sat on the chair nearest to Heather, who was still deeply engaged in coloring the cookies. Her tongue was licking back and forth over her upper lip as though that motion belonged to the success of sprinkling the colored sugars.

"Heather?"

"Uh huh."

"Heather." This time, Claire spoke louder.

Quick to respond to the merest sense of trouble, Heather immediately looked up and stared into Claire's face. The sprinkling container was arrested in midair.

Claire lifted the bag then opened it so Heather could see inside.

A wide smile spread across Heather's face. "Patti likes me now Aunt Claire." Only recently had Heather exchanged her 'Mama' to 'Aunt Claire'. Claire had let it go without talking about the change because she wanted what was natural for Heather in terms of addressing her. "Patti never let me play dolls or tea with her and her friends. Now, she said I can come to the next party. Isn't that nice?"

So Heather had bought her way into a group by pleasing the leader with gifts.

Bribes work. Even a fuzzy pink sweater opens doors formerly closed.

Claire knew Heather did not understand that Patti was only a guise of a friend, and that this false friend could trick Heather into taking any or all of her belongings. Heather's concern was to make Patti happy, even to handing over all of her beloved items.

"Let me tell you something that is very important, Heather."

Heather put down her sprinkling shaker. As the moon eclipses the sun, she lost her sunny disposition and a solemn darkness moved across her face.

"A true friend will give as much as she takes. If the giving is only toward her, then she is not a friend. Patti fooled you so she could take your things. A real friend would never do that.

"It is wonderful that you have a big kind heart, Heather, but sometimes people will pretend to like you only to get what they want from you. Patti seems like a nice girl, but she has something inside of her that will take from other people even when she shouldn't. Do you understand?"

Scrunching up her mouth, "Sort of," escaped from a corner opening. Then a sudden bright exuberance filled her. "I get it, Aunt Claire!"

"Good! Now how about we finish decorating the cookies then make an apple pie?"

Dessert smells filled the kitchen and reached with tendrils throughout the house. In the kitchen, lighting shone down on them like Bethlehem stars. Their chatter seemed to color the walls in gaiety and springtime, when the beauty of nature opens her colors of purple, yellow and white.

Chapter Three

One day in Heather's sixth grade year, she burst through the front door after school. "Aunt Claire! Aunt Claire!"

"In the kitchen, Heather!"

Stomping into the yellow daisy-papered kitchen, Heather plopped her books atop the long maple rectangular table in the breakfast nook, then sprawled into an adjoining chair. Her face was florid. Claire knew Heather's light complexion flushed only when agitated or embarrassed. She guessed which of these it was and stopped her food preparations for dinner. Joining Heather at the table she waited quietly.

Heather stared at the tabletop but her inner mood was evident by her fingers drumming loudly on the table's surface.

Claire knew it would be a while, so she pondered Heather's profile as she waited. It matched her mother's. The nose was a superlative concave shape and wrinkled, as her mother's had, when she laughed. Heather's long eyelashes were the same as Jeanette's also, and swept up, nearly to her eyebrows. These eyes were the exact amber eyes of her mother, though unlike her mother, Heather's lips were full, like her father's, with a dip in the center of the top lip.

Also from her father, Heather had inherited a large forehead but it was covered by her red bangs. Her hair hung to her shoulders in natural loose ruddy curls.

The only part of her facial composition Claire didn't understand was one dimple at the top of her right cheekbone. When Heather laughed, this little gap appeared and was charming in its showing.

Already, Claire knew Heather was attractive and would draw much attention from boys. Yet what kept Claire's thinking more occupied was her hope that Heather would be beautiful on the inside. Claire understood which the greater gift was.

Finally, unable to wait any longer, Claire broke the silence. "Tell me what's happened, Heather." She cupped her hands

22

around Heather's to still their nervous drumming.

Heather looked up, her eyes now glistening with tears. "Sharlene and her friends beat me up!"

"What!"

"They waited in the bushes and jumped at me. They made a circle and Sharlene shoved me around inside the ring. She pushed me to the ground then sat on my back and rubbed my face in the grass while they all laughed! It was terrible, Aunt Claire!" she nearly yelled, then broke into unrestrained sobbing.

In an instant Claire was to her, holding her, rocking her, repeating, "Shh, shh." She could feel the high temperature in Heather's young distraught body, but she let it go on; this authentic storm of life.

When the outburst abated, Heather looked at her aunt and declared with no small amount of rancor, "I don't know what Sharlene's problem is!" She wiped the tears from her eyes and cheeks, and sniffed loudly between sentences as she shared, "She likes Tony and says he's her boyfriend, but Tony says I'm his girlfriend, Aunt Claire." Another fresh flow of tears began as Heather resolutely cried, "And I don't like either one of them!" Claire let this squall run its course. "She even kicked me!" Heather ended with dudgeon, then lifted her yellow dress bottom to show Claire a large swelling bruise below her left knee. "They were yelling, 'Orphan! Orphan!' the whole time. Finally, an adult came by and they ran away. The woman helped me home." Heather's lower lip was quivering. "Why did they do that to me, Aunt Claire?"

"Come with me. We'll sit in the living room and talk about this." She urged Heather to their soft-cushioned white sofa and there they sat in a huddle. "Have you heard the word, 'jealousy'?" Claire asked.

"Yes," Heather answered, sniffing, and sweeping the last vestige of tears from her now red puffy eyes.

"Sharlene is jealous of you, which means she wants what you have; namely Tony."

"But I don't want Tony!"

"But he wants you, and Sharlene wants him to want her, so you have what she wants. That makes her hit you and kick you and call you names."

"What good does that do?"

"None at all."

"Then why does she do it?"

How could Claire tell this emerging young woman about greed and how the world grabbed for its portion plus the shares of others? What words could convey how desperate and cruel could be the human clawing, and how material and ruthless people become to get things, and yet are never satisfied? "First of all, you are a pretty girl and lots of boys besides Tony will like you only because of the way you look. Let's pretend, and say you are both pretty and also act like Sharlene. Would Tony and other boys like you then?"

Heather looked at her wide-eyed, ruminating on these words. She didn't answer because she was too young to understand.

Claire pushed the hair back from her niece's broad forehead and kissed her softly there before continuing. "The answer, Heather, is 'Yes'. Lots of boys would still like you, even if you act horrid. They will like you simply because you are pretty."

"Yuck!"

"Many doors will open in your life because of it you are nice-looking. Sharlene wants beauty, and she can't have it, so she will try and get what she wants another way, even if it means hurting others. She may never learn how wrong that is. Many people live a lifetime without understanding the difference between right and wrong. They injure people in less obvious ways than jumping at them from the bushes, but when those people want something, whatever or whoever is in their way becomes something to use or get rid of. I'm sorry this happened." She looked into the perplexed amber eyes of her niece. "Sometimes, Heather, the greatest lessons in life are learned in these hard ways. Sharlene is an example of what not to become. She is to be pitied, not hated." Claire embraced Heather. "Do you feel a little better now?"

"A little."

"Good enough to concentrate on your homework, while I call your teacher and let her know what's happened?"

Heather pulled away. "Aunt Claire! Please don't!"

"Your teacher must be told. When we are involved in something this wrong, we have to speak out."

Heather flopped against the back cushions and stared at the opposite wall. Taking a deep breath and sliding out her lower lip, she exhaled, causing her red bangs to blow up and stand vertical in their center for a moment. "You're right, Aunt Claire, my teacher should know."

Claire watched closely as Heather came and went the following weeks. The outward behavior seemed the same, with her young red-headed niece hastening in all directions, but Claire sensed a barely perceptible something about Heather. Soberness is all she knew what to call it, as though a serious grain of sand had lodged within the oyster's shell and a tiny pearl had begun to form.

"Can I come, Aunt Claire?"

"May I come," Claire corrected.

"May I come?"

Heather's agreeable nature was a comfortable fit as plans and directions were arranged every day in their home. That easy submission, however, was also a point of concern for Claire regarding her niece. Claire knew skill was needed to avoid trouble in the world awaiting Heather, because "yes" could become an echo between the squeezing walls of a dangerous night. The beauty emerging in her would require discernment to handle the lusting certain to come her way. She would need to say, "no," and to say it firmly, but so far, "yes" was Heather's most visceral response.

Claire had lost track of the "yes" times Heather had volunteered; to care for the classroom pet for the summer, or "yes, I'll take the bird with the broken leg and fix it," and "yes, the stray cat can come home with me." Her caring was a virtue, but Claire knew the world's wolf could come to Heather dissembled under the guise of a helpless lamb.

They wrapped two roasted chickens and put them on separate paper plates. Next to each golden chicken they nestled two capped plastic containers. One held Claire's homemade breaded dressing, and the other was filled with gravy devised from the roasting process. Heather scotch-taped yellow and orange ribbons, wound into bows, atop each package. Claire enjoyed watching Heather's concentration to achieve her decorative addition at the very center of each covered chicken.

"We have four stops today," Claire offered as she carefully lowered the offerings into a large plastic food container. These excursions into the community were possible and integral to Claire's life because she was financially solvent. The hierarchy of needs, even with the expense of raising Heather, were easily met, leaving her caring personality free to express itself. Claire's husband, a man older than she, had been a doctor and passed away at the young age of sixty from complications of Alzheimer's disease. Those hard frustrating years of watching Oliver slip from a gifted surgeon to a stumbling vacancy were harsh and cruel. Somehow she had survived.

At first Claire had taken on an assortment of social activities; the group for Bridge once a week, golfing, tennis, but they seemed frivolous to her and she soon dropped her participation in each activity.

As though developing a relationship with loneliness was the only way to understand and begin to expiate that fiend, Claire took on a quest to minister to the lonely. She had been at this new way of life several years when Heather came to her so unexpectedly, but Claire had been able to make ample room for Heather while continuing to reach into her community as both Redeemed and Redeemer.

Heather selection of clothing was a green dress with large brass buttons at the bottom of the sleeves. Claire had encouraged her to compliment the color of her red hair by the use of greens and browns and yellows when she made choices about what to wear. Heather enjoyed lingering over selections for her day's combination of garments. Already, her understanding of personal appearance was acute. Claire understood that the awakened sense of making herself as attractive as possible was not so much from a sense of personal satisfaction as it was from a desire to be agreeable and approved by others.

In a world where only principles of physical and moral laws from out of creation's primordial chaos could indeed be realized in absolute ways by the tonnage of humankind today, then Heather would be safe. But Claire knew better. She had no guarantee for Heather's security with her youthful innocence and vulnerability. Even the incident with Sharlene, sobering as it had been for Heather, had left the majority of this youthful redhead as effulgent and trusting as ever.

Their first stop was the hospital. They crossed a busy street that placed them on a sidewalk leading to the entrance of the square, four-story white building. Off to the right, a long rectangular garden of well-tended, variously-colored Roses cheered their way, but a feeling of yellowing met the senses upon entering through the heavy front glass doors. The only human present was an aged woman as yellow as the faded walls, who sat below the level of the countertop. She was occupied with a large binder propped on a stand. When she noticed them, she creaked a question about how she might help.

Claire had felt Heather's hand tighten around her own the moment they entered the hospital and now it palpitated noticeably.

Whispering as they walked away, Claire asked if she was okay.

"It smells funny in here."

"Hospitals have sickness and healing in them. Isn't it wonderful to live at a time when so much can be done to help people who are sick?"

As always, Heather agreed, but she didn't loosen her firm grasp upon her aunt's hand.

They joined an elderly couple in a third floor room. The husband, while recovering from one surgery, had fallen and broken a hip and this morning had undergone another surgery to repair the mishap. His wife, a tiny white-haired woman with a doll face and crystal-blue eyes, sat by his bedside and never loosened her tremulous hold upon her husband's large vein-bulging hand. "Claire, you are so thoughtful to think about us." With her one free hand she began to fumble in her purse. "I'll get the key for our front door." She withdrew a set of keys, attempting to extract one particular large brass-colored key.

Immediately, Heather released her hold on Claire, asking, "May I help you?" Her generous curls of red hair bent next to the thin white hair of the wife as Heather followed directions on how to release the key.

"The woman addressed Heather. "Would you do me a big favor?"

"Yes."

"I have a friend named George. He's a twenty-year-old bird called a Cockatoo. Would you give him some birdseed and tell him we love him and I'll be home soon?"

Heather looked wide and fully into the pale blue eyes. "Yes, I'd like that!"

Arrangements for placing the front door key under a potted plant in a side garden were concluded and the little wife offered another profusion of thank-you's for helping in their time of need. The husband hadn't opened his eyes throughout this visit, but he breathed loudly through his nose with positive regularity.

Chapter Four

They pulled to a stop in front of a small home with a worn-out look. Made of wood, it seemed hardly more than a heap of planks nailed together. The concrete walk leading to the front porch was short and cracked, but swept clean. An ancient Magnolia tree sat as the sole resident in the small well-trimmed grassy patch of front yard. Its size affirmed a life of duration and, for this early fall season, once again it offered red-seeded candelabras standing thickly upon the shiny leaf body. Like a mother giving birth year after year to others of her kind, her seeds fell by the thousands in hopes a few would catch and know life. Claire and Heather stopped a moment to admire its beauty.

"See how God arranges life, Heather? He made this tree to have all these seeds to assure at least some would survive and carry on the species. That's how you came to life also. There were thousands of possibilities when you were created, but you alone were the one to come into the world."

Heather smiled in appreciation.

The interior of the house was small, faded, and clean. The sofa sagged, telling the observer that two bodies often inhabited spots right next to one another.

Heather busied herself with George who sang lustily in response to Heather's chattering around his cage, while Claire opened the refrigerator to place the roast meal inside. As always with her visits to this elderly couple, she found the refrigerator nearly bare. She called Heather to her side.

Heather moved across the room continuing a brisk conversation with George, until she came up alongside her aunt. She looked into the refrigerator. "Why is it empty?"

"They are old and poor," Claire answered.

"You mean they don't have enough money for food?"

"They have enough government aid to eat modestly, but getting to a store and the work of cooking is difficult at their age."

29

Heather's eyes met her aunt's then returned to the empty refrigerator. "They didn't look hungry."

"It's not that bad, Heather, but they struggle to do what comes easy for us. There are millions of people who suffer this way."

"Then why don't more people help them and cook for them?"

Claire shut the refrigerator door. "Remember how Sharlene treated you?"

An aggrieved darkness passed over Heather's face and her plump lips tightened. She shook her head up and down, causing her shiny red hair to bounce.

"Sharlene wants to take, not to give. I'm sorry to say that many people are selfish and care only about themselves; not all people, thank goodness, but most."

As they left, Heather slipped the key under the designated pot then cooed her good-byes to George.

Walking toward their car, Claire put her arm around Heather. "The world is always made better by helping others less fortunate than we. Remember that, Heather."

They made additional stops and another food delivery for that day, each recipient in obvious need of one type or another.

Dear Aunt Claire,

I know its not Mothers Day. But I want to tell you about last week. When I was a little girl I wanted to grow up and be Annie Oakley. I thought that place in Nevada where mom and dad died would be a nice place to have a horse and ride for the pony express. But I know the pony express is over. Ive been thinking since our trip to deliver the chickens last week. All the girls want to be models and movie actreses. They call me 'bah bah black sheep' because my hero is dead. Its true that Annie Oakley lived forever ago. I try to be like them and want to be a famous actres but it doesnt work. But now it will be easier on me because I can tell them I no longer want to be Annie Oakley. Now I want to be Florence Nightingale; I mean I want to be like her. Im glad you changed me by showing me people who need help. Ill let you know how the girls take it. Maybe they wont call me 'bah bah black sheep' any more.

love,
Heather

Heather's letters were always found in the mornings next to Claire's coffee maker. They had evolved into a confessional. From the start, these communications had been candid, but more importantly, the inner musings from the red-haired one, fermented and came to fruition by way of these written sharings. Claire knew Heather was sensitive and also that she was frequently troubled about being accepted and liked. Love is required. Without touch the infant dies. To love and be loved is the dearest waltz of every life.

One day at lunch, Claire's friend, Rose, a psychiatrist by training, advised, "Heather's empty spot is desertion. Even though her mom and dad died in an auto wreck, Heather's deeper, unconscious thinking interprets that as abandonment. The threat of being deserted is of paramount concern to a young personality when important people in that life have died unexpectedly."

"But Heather was only an infant," Claire protested.

"Yes. But she grew up and learned the story."

"You mean I shouldn't have told her?"

Rose looked with astonishment at Claire. "If I didn't know you better I'd suggest you make an appointment to see me on a professional basis! Claire Summers you are a woman of truth and we both know that!" A wry smile bent one side of Rose's lean face tilting her heart-shaped lips. Behind thickened glasses, her eyes sparkled. "Heather could overreact to rejection because she lost her parents. It doesn't matter how superhuman a job you do to raise her, the fact remains she lives in a peopled world where children are supposed to have a mother and a father. If they differ from that expected pattern, they can become pariahs in the eyes of their peers. Consequently, Heather could grab acceptance from deleterious quarters. That is my only warning."

"What can I do?"

"Watch her friends. Keep her with good ones." Rose leaned forward, lowering her voice, "Heather will grow up as sure as God made little green apples and she will carry her extraordinary

31

need for approval a long time before she grows wise enough to understand and temper it. You won't always be there to help her."

"Prayers. The Covert of Wings. The High Tower. The Mighty Fortress. Incense."

"Beg pardon?"

"Prayers, Rose, you know those things we do when we get on our knees and bring our hands together and with open hearts supplicate to God?"

Rose chuckled. "I look in a textbook for what you look for on your knees. Maybe between those two, Heather will make the right choices and stay out of trouble."

The ladies finished their meal within a dining room growing more and more jocular this Friday afternoon. The passage leading to and from the dining room passed the bar area where colorful stacks of bottled liquors were lit from behind. When they arrived, there were two customers inside the bar. Now, two hours later, every stool was filled and a heavy cloud of cigarette and tobacco smoke hung in the room above the vinous chatter.

"Odd," Rose commented when they were outside, "how the bar conversation often ends in dispute, but the crowd returns again, like a moth to the flame, to be killed a little bit more."

"Why do they do it?"

"Some people believe life is too demanding, or their inner world is conflicted, or their perceived deficiencies frighten them, so they drink to escape. They associate being drunk with being free. Plus, there's that innate rebellion in our human nature that causes some people to reject good decisions in favor of bad ones just because they can.

"Of course, it's floundering and destructive but at bars they find people with the same needs and together they enjoy a brief pleasant, but false, reality." With her heart-shaped mouth, Rose smiled warmly at Claire. "May I share a professional secret with you?"

"One of my virtues is that I can be trusted," Claire responded.

"My psychiatric profession flourishes. Often, instead of pills for depression, and pills for insomnia, and loops and loops of discussions about the same things, it comes right down to problems with mother and father, especially mother." Rose hesitated, shaking her head before continuing, "I can't count the times I've thought we only need to see and contemplate the backward E of Saturn to be mentally healthy."

The statement confused Claire and she realized it must have shown because Rose's full mouth, in that small thin face with cupid lips, took on its wry twist. "Ah! Perplexity! That suggests you can be guided."

How Claire loved this clever intelligent friend. How many truths flow into our lives every day? How many are gathered? How many are lost?

"It works like this," Rose continued, "the 'backward E of Saturn' is the key. There is momentary confusion of your mental consciousness while you are giving full attention to the unexpected statement, 'backward E of Saturn.' Your conscious mind becomes occupied with searching for some previous experience similar to the idea so you will know how to respond. Meanwhile, your unconscious mind is without its protection, and in that unguarded state suggestions can be pushed into your mind. It's a technique of brainwashing, and in my opinion an unethical practice."

"An unfair advantage not taken cancels an unfair advantage. It's all about choices," Claire answered.

"Claire, you are not my friend without good reason!"

Claire slipped her arm around the thin arm of her friend as they walked back to her station wagon.

"The answer," Rose continued, "is not brainwashing, but simplicity. I'm certain that high-powered telescopes trained to the night-sky and a law requiring all citizens of the world to use them fifteen minutes every night before bedtime would radically change individuals and world politics. Think, Claire, of the awesome magnitude of the Milky Way with its uncountable crowded starry reality, and the beauty and fact of fixed design." Rose swept her free arm through the air as though to encompass eternity. "The mysterious reality is forever, with earth less than an atom in our endless universe. If we contemplate that profound reality, our problems are rendered less significant, don't you agree?"

"Maybe we can't overcome the tendency to think small."

"It's true that many people wouldn't look at the rings of

Saturn unless you paid them. Yet, in spite of that, I believe the marvel would impact even the dullest among us, and make humans wiser about existence. My goodness, look at that, Claire!"

The two middle-aged friends; one slim, dark and tall, and somewhat frail; the other not as tall, and slightly plump, linked arm in arm as they stopped at the edge of the town's central square. "Ginkgo biloba," Claire noted, "the first tree known to mankind. It's a slow grower so this tree must be hundreds of years old."

They lingered silently beneath the venerable towering umbrella with its 14-Karat gold colored leaves shaped like tiny fans. A breeze caused the giant plant to ripple its countless adornments in little swingings.

"How does it make you feel?" Claire asked, indicating the tree.

"Calm and amazed, and if a tree in a park can do that, think what the rings of Saturn could do."

Dear Aunt Claire,

I've decided 6th grade is neat. I'm not sure I like my red hair because I get teased about it so much. Johnnie likes me and I like him too except he has a dumb laugh. I don't think I'll go steady with him because that laugh would bother me so much I might not like him as much as I do now. I'm pretty sure I'll say 'no'. He's suppose to ask me this Friday if I want to go steady with him. I like Ken better anyway. Ken is real quiet and tall. His hair is black and curly.

Once he said he liked my red hair but he never asks to walk with me after school. Cindy said to flutter my eyes at him and smile as big as I can. I tried that but he just looked at me funny and kept walking. Do you have any ideas on how to make him like me?

Love,
heather
p.s. I like my name with a little 'h'. What do you think?

Claire sat at her desk in front of dozens of paper piles representing community organizations reaching out to people in

34

need. From that mammoth desk, she connected the two in benignant fashion.

Luxurious red hair appeared around Claire's right shoulder. Heather kissed her aunt on the cheek. "Hi, Aunt Claire."

"Hi. How was school?" Claire pushed away from the desk, resting her attention on Heather.

"School is fine, it's Ken who is awful." Plopping her books onto the floor, Heather landed her young agile body into the padded Birdseye maple chair next to Claire's desk. Their talking, as usual, was face to face.

Heather's brow wrinkled and her lips, pressed hard together, twisted to one side. Her amber eyes studied the floor as though the well-worn and richly shining oak planks were an item of great concern to her. "I don't get it, Aunt Claire."

Claire ignored the papers she had been working on pertaining to a young divorced mother of two who was recovering from chemotherapy and in need of child-care. For these moments, Heather would have her full attention. "What don't you get?"

Shaking her head, Heather continued, "I've done everything. I've let his friends know I like him. I tried the stupid eye flutter thing and I smile my best whenever I see him. Oh, Aunt Claire, if you only knew how I feel inside just to see him. He's so neat."

"Are we talking about Ken?"

"Yes, he's the only one for me. And you know what's really strange? When I'm around him I can't think of one thing to say!"

Claire didn't answer because she knew Heather wasn't finished.

"He's handsome and strong, but he doesn't talk much. He never says more than a few words at a time, and his voice is real low and soft. Do you think that means I like the strong silent type?"

Still Claire didn't respond because Heather had only taken a breath in her voluble stream.

"He doesn't have a girlfriend and only one other girl likes him." Here Heather paused and looked at her aunt. "Guess who?" she asked, a look of disgust covering her face.

"Sharlene?"

"Yes! Can you believe the meanest person on earth would like Ken too?" Now Heather kept her attention on Claire's face and spoke no more. Claire knew she was ready for a response.

"Sharlene likes him for the simple reason that she knows you like him. She's still jealous of you. Though aside from that, in sixth grade, it should be obvious if Ken likes you or if not you, then who?"

"It's possible he likes Pam. But can't I make him like me, Aunt Claire? My girlfriends say you can make a boy like you if you flirt. What does that mean?"

"Flirting means to tease a boy sexually, but that's not the kind of 'liking' you want, Heather. That kind never lasts and everyone ends up unhappy. The only way to find the right boy is to be yourself. He has to like you the way you are."

"But Ken won't notice me if I do that!"

"Then Ken isn't the boy for you."

"But he's super, Aunt Claire. He even walks cute; sort of bow-legged like a cowboy. I wish I could get him to hold my hand after school."

Not wanting to sound pedantic, Claire wondered how she could tell Heather there would be more disappointments and that life wasn't life without them, but that there were also triumphs and dreams that come true. She answered, "I thought I was in love with my high school sweetheart, Vic. He finished high school two years ahead of me, joined the Air Force, and was sent overseas to Japan. All I did in my spare time after homework was write long letters to him. Then at night I would put a big red X on a calendar I had over my bed which meant one more day was over and Vic was that much closer to coming home on what they call a 'furlough', which means something like a little vacation. Time moved so slowly it felt like it wasn't moving at all." Claire gave a gusty laugh. "And thank goodness I didn't marry him because I found out later that he had a girlfriend in Japan and they had a child together. He left both of them in Japan when he returned to the United States."

"How horrible!"

"Yes, isn't it? He was writing me letters about the parties he went to and saying how much of a wallflower he was. He said he stood in the corner and watched everyone else, and I believed him! The truth came out later that he had so many girlfriends it's amazing he could keep track of them. All those months I was sure I loved him and had waited faithfully, but when I saw him, it felt different. Not too much later, when I found out about his girlfriends, it made sense why things were changed between us. He wanted to get engaged, but I said 'no'. If I had said 'yes', my life would never have been happy. Instead, a few years later I met and married your Uncle Oliver. He and I had a deeply committed and loving marriage. So you see? Sometimes things work out better even when it isn't what we think we want."

"You mean I should give up Ken?"

"If he hasn't liked you back after all this time, he probably never will."

"But I want him to like me!"

"Ken may never feel about you the way you want him to feel. But there will be a right boy for you, Heather, for certain there will be, you just haven't met him yet."

Heather's amber eyes stared blankly. Without another word she picked up her schoolbooks and trudged into her bedroom shutting the door softly behind herself. She didn't come out for dinner and no light shone from under her door. Claire knew she was resolving matters of the heart, and gave her privacy for this most delicate and important time in a young developing life.

Dear Aunt Claire,

You are so neat to write to, even better than my diary. First of all, you were right about Ken. I stopped noticing him or at least pretended to, even though my heart still pounded every time he was near. I had to work not to think about him two rows back during Social Studies. Eachday gets better. Mary, a friend of mine from Home Ec., said she has heard of girls getting a boy this way! That is too weird! She said she tried it on Sam and it worked. All she did was act like she didn't care about him and then he started walking her home after school. Now they are going steady. If I live to be a million years old, I will never understand this stuff. Anyway, Ken isn't like Sam. I don't think he's even noticed that I'm not watching him all the time now. That must mean he really and truly does not like me for a girlfriend. To be honest, Aunt Claire, I feel kind of dumb to have liked him so much when he didn't care about me.

Want to hear something even weirder? Sharlene stopped liking him the same day I did. I still hear her tell peeple she hates red hair.
Do you think my red hair is why Ken didn't like me?
Love,

heather...Heather

p.s. I still can't decide if I like a small h or a big H.

"Yes, her grades are excellent," Claire offered in answer to Rose's question at their weekly luncheon. This friendship stretched now over a decade, to the time when Claire lost her husband to Alzheimer's disease. Claire credited Rose for commiseration with her deep and horrid grief during the years following Oliver's death. True, Rose was a psychiatrist, but first she was Claire's friend.

Rose herself had a cross to bear after her youngest son, Christopher, accidentally swallowed medication at a toddling age and became severely brain damaged. Claire learned about this sorrow in Rose's family, and how all six of her family members had decided to keep the little disabled boy as part of their family unit. Christopher could walk, but he talked only in guttural ways. The family members understood a little of the child's speech. Gradually, Rose and her family had reconciled with the tragedy and met the day-to-day challenges of caring for a helpless, dependant child.

Many times, Rose would talk about not wasting time on things that can't be changed because what happens in life happens. "At first," Rose confided, "I took all the guilt, because they were my pills. I was away from Christopher talking to one of my patients on the phone. But I know human goodness can be lost and wasted over feelings of guilt. I see it every day. Guilt is a healthy reminder to do better next time, but it can hang on too long and paralyze a personality. So, I didn't blame myself unreasonably. I accepted the situation and determined to do the best with it that I possibly could. Christopher is clearly a happy child. It's we adults who understand the price of the accident. Until Judgment Day I won't understand why accidents like

Christopher's and Heather's parents happen to some and not to others." Rose pulled her heart shaped lips into her tilted smile. "Meanwhile, I'll have a Caesar's salad, how about you?"

For Claire, that particular luncheon, long ago, stood out because it was the first time Rose had opened her secrets. It marked a change in their friendship. Afterwards, their relationship had grown deeper and more meaningful because they now shared, uncensored, the situations of their lives and fully trusted one another with those private sensitivities.

Today, at their weekly luncheon, they were discussing Heather. "Yes, last quarter her grades were all A's except for Math. She had a D in fractions."

"Is Ken in her math class?"

"That's the only class they share."

"That could be why. How long has she been 'off Ken', shall we call it?"

Claire drummed the white tablecloth with her fingers and looked over Rose's shoulder to the wall with old black and white photographs of local pioneers. "About two months," she estimated.

"A sixth grader is not very dogged, so her grieving will be over any day. They don't have the mental acumen to stay fixed on a lost boyfriend for long. Even if Ken had liked her back and they went steady, I've never known a couple at this age to go on and make their golden anniversary. A few reach it when they connect in high school, but rarely any sooner. It's all part of the maturing process. You and I could tell Heather about life fifty different ways, and still she would ignore what we said, and struggle and suffer to learn that same information on her own. Most of us do the same thing at Heather's age. But she will fly back from her heartache any day. Meanwhile, keep an eye on the math, if it doesn't improve, you may need to get some tutoring."

Dear Aunt Claire,

Guess What? A new boy came into my math class. He sits four rows over from me, at the last row under the window. His name is Donald. He has blond hair and his front teeth are a little bit too big, but he's real cute. And guess what? (I already said that) He smiles at me a lot, and he doesn't smile at the other girls. I wonder if that means he thinks I'm cute and doesn't mind red hair? I hardly thought about Ken all day.

Love,
heather...Heather

p.s. I got an A in fractions today.

What buoyant happiness this niece, Heather, brought her, Claire mused, as she sat at her desk over a list of volunteers on-call regarding the delivery of food to shut-ins.

Frequently, Claire pondered the mystery that her sister, Jeanette, and brother-in-law, Mark, were gone. They would not see their daughter grow up. They would not see her wrestle with Jacob and climb the ascending way. They would not see the twirling layers of pink and white that define the open shell and the feast.

Now a seventh grader, Heather was blossoming with the promise of slim, well-formed ankles and calves, freckles along her arms, an concave nose, a dimple atop her right cheek, and large amber eyes, all crowned by the glory of her thick red wavy hair. It was obvious that she was blossoming into a beautiful woman. Claire also knew Heather's uncertainty about her red hair would, in time, become appreciation. In a world of mainly brown and dark-haired people, red becomes valued simply for its rarity. Conversely, if red heads abounded, the occasional brown adorned head would be coveted. Because of this intrinsic nature, we get gold for glass beads.

It was a Thursday afternoon, a neon-blue-skied day in October, when the chrysanthemums were a tall reddish-purple forest on both sides of the meandering shale walkway up to the concrete steps at the front entrance to their home. Claire was at her desk, arranging emergency rent for a destitute single mother of two who had been brought to America from Vietnam by a soldier, then deserted. She heard Heather already calling, "Aunt Claire! Aunt Claire!" even before the front screen door opened. Alarmed, Claire quickly spun to face Heather's beaming seventh grade face, with its set of metal braces holding captive every tooth in her mouth. Claire was pleased to see such an unabashed smile since Heather had taken to smiling without opening her lips, causing a distorted expression. "Look!" Heather proudly held up an ungainly ring on a long silver necklace that resembled a braid.

Now she understood the emergency. "I think someone likes you."

"Yes! And guess who?"

Claire contemplated the vicissitude of Heather's boyfriend changes. Donald was a Roger and a Tim ago. Maybe it was Jack. That was a name bandied around lately at dinnertime. "Jack?"

"Oh, Aunt Claire, you are so right! He gave me his ring today! He's the first boy to ask me to go steady since these." Heather pointed to her braces and wrinkled her nose in disgust.

"Congratulations!"

"Everybody knows we are each other's boyfriend and girlfriend. We're serious about each other."

"What do you mean by 'serious', Heather?"

"Aunt Claire! You know; he kisses me sometimes, like today at the bridge on our way home."

"Well, if you like him, he must be a very nice boy."

"He's the neatest!"

Claire smiled, but determined to appraise the situation more deeply after the confidence about the kissing. "What about Jack do you like most?"

"He's tall."

Claire waited. "And?"

"He has curly blond hair." Heather dumped her schoolbooks onto the long plush couch and skipped into the kitchen. Claire heard the refrigerator door open.

"I made a pumpkin pie today, fresh from a pumpkin. It's on the second shelf, and there's a can of whipped cream in the refrigerator door."

"Neat," was all Claire heard from within the depths of the refrigerator. She waited the moments, listening to her niece's progress. A few minutes later, Heather appeared with a large slice of pumpkin pie and a balancing feat of whipped cream layered atop it. She slipped into the chair next to Claire then

41

fixed her attention on the effort to obtain a bite. "This is neat, Aunt Claire."

"Thank you. So Jack is tall and blond?"

"Yes, he's neat."

"Is there something more about him that you like?"

"Sally thinks he's a good kisser, but I think his lower lip is kinda fat."

"So he's tall, and blond, and maybe a good kisser, and has a sort of fat lower lip. Anything else?"

A serious expression settled over Heather's face. "He whispered in my ear that he doesn't mind my braces."

Now Claire knew she had the truest cause for this union. Jack had accepted Heather, braces and all. "He sounds like a winner, Heather."

The phone rang, causing Heather to quickly deposit her pie plate on the edge of Claire's desk and flee to the ringing, as she chirped, "That's Jack, he said he'd call in half an hour." She disappeared behind the door of her lacy bedroom, after which only muffled peals of giggling came forth into Claire's hearing.

Maybe he's the reliable sort, Claire pondered. At least he calls when he says he'll call.

Claire returned to her business of arranging the paperwork plan to care for the Vietnamese woman and her children. There would be emergency aid, then a referral to a Catholic charities organization where they helped immigrants to learn English and receive training for employment.

Heather's door slammed and she appeared in a gush back into the neighboring chair. Retrieving her pumpkin pie, she spoke enthusiastically of Jack between bites. "He especially likes my red hair, and there's a dance at the school next Friday and he wants to take me. Isn't that neat?" Before Claire could answer, Heather was on her feet. Claire heard the plate go into the sink with a clatter before Heather reappeared, scooped up her books, and hurried into her bedroom. The door shut with a crash.

"Hormones," Claire murmured.

Chapter Five

"Rose," Claire began, at their luncheon, as they were about to begin their same choice of veal scaloppini, "What are the kids doing with and to each other these days?"

"The age of innocence is dead."

"That bad?"

"Probably. I know you've seen the preponderance of sex and violence on television." A healthy competent professional woman, Rose usually kept a benevolent comportment with the world. Everything she said was with a good-natured and appealing emotional quality. Seldom was it that she took on a somber appearance but this time, Claire saw anger flash in her hazel eyes as she continued, "Nowhere in human history has the violence of youth been as notable as it is now, when kids listen to rude musical lyrics and live in front of television sets that teach nefarious morals toward females and gratuitous violence day after day. This is senseless violence I'm talking about, without meaning or provocation or justification. Today's kids are violent for the sake of violence and frankly, I'm worried."

Rose's serious side was typically conveyed with a twinkling in her eyes and a smile that seemed to run effortlessly throughout her entire body. Always, Claire marveled at the heartfelt acceptance and appreciation of life that Rose projected. Whether of sorrow or joy, she seemed to understand the nature of humanity and accepted both its caresses and its blows. But today was different.

"Have you ever heard of the Bo-Bo Doll?" Rose continued.

Claire stared at the paneled ceiling a moment, searching her memory in this vault-like room where they were taking lunch, then answered, "No, I can't remember ever hearing that name before."

"The Bo-Bo Doll is an adult size balloon clown with a sanded bottom. It's a replica of a clown, with smiling red lips, yellow hair poking out from under a small derby hat, and clown eyes,

43

just the way you see them at a circus. If you pull the Bo-Bo Doll down then release it, the clown pops upright again because of its round weighted bottom.

"Psychologists have demonstrated the transference of violent behavior to children by using this Bo-Bo Doll. They divided children into two groups. The first group is shown a film of various activities taking place in the room where the Bo-Bo Doll sits, but no one in the film pays any attention to the doll. After the movie the children are let into the same room the film showed. The people in the film acted as though the Bo-Bo Doll wasn't there, and now the children act the same way. They ignore the Bo-Bo Doll.

"The second group of children are shown a different film, and this time the adults go over and punch the Bo-Bo Doll. When it pops up, it gets punched again. The Bo-Bo Doll getting pounded is the main activity in the room. When the film is over, this group of children is released into that room and immediately they go up to the Bo-Bo Doll and start swinging. Most of their time and attention are taken up by beating on the Bo-Bo Doll," Rose concluded.

"So violence is learned by mimicking?"

"Potently."

Tabula rasa must be filled with that which presents itself. The tablets will forever struggle with the taint passed along as the living social code.

Rose continued, "There's nothing we can do about it and that's the most frustrating part for me. Even though I don't believe in the innate goodness of humanity, in whichever culture it happens to find itself, I believe its excellent parts are being crushed little by little. Today, you visit lands where people still live in caves and there will be a TV antenna atop the opening. You win a national beauty contest in Russia and your prize is a television set. Like a meltdown, it can't be stopped. It's everywhere on the planet; it's in the air we breathe." She paused, thoughtfully piercing her fork into a piece of veal. "Did you know that 90% of all television viewing material watched in the world is produced in Hollywood? Thematically, that means film #2 of the Bo-Bo Doll plays over and over, with a preponderance of sexual gratuity thrown into the brainwash." Rose shook her head, causing Claire to notice the high shine on Rose's tight brown curls with their hint of gray. "For the first time in history children are watching thousands of staged murders and uncensored sex and violence every day on television and in movies and through music, and when we're told kids in America are senselessly violent for the first time in our history, people wonder why. As a race, we are pitiful in terms of perception, don't you agree, Claire?"

"I do."

The two friends shrugged at one another, then fell to eating their lunch.

"One last thing, regarding Heather," Rose finished, "Anything is possible, so remember to watch who she chooses for her friends, and keep her boundaries clear."

For the Friday night dance Heather would attend with Jack, Claire volunteered to be a chaperone. It took Heather eight hours to prepare. She wore a blue satin dress that had a large bow at the back of the waist with trailing ribbons to the bottom of the hem. For shoes, she chose silver flats with rhinestones sparkling across the top. Prior to dressing, she strolled through the garden and selected small rosebuds from their white rose trees. These were carefully put aside in the refrigerator until now. With a satin rustle, Heather appeared from her room. Her hair was partially piled atop her head with the remaining scarlet hanging down her back. Blue eye shadow had been applied to her eyelids and pink rouge tinged her cheeks. A slightly red lipstick complimented her full mouth.

Stiffly, Heather walked to the refrigerator, delicately lifting the rosebuds, then just as robot-like returned to her room and shut the door. When she next appeared, the white rosebuds had been cleverly embedded into her curly red hair, edifying its beauty.

When Jack arrived, his parents waited outside in their family car. Heather's introduction of him had been formal and awkward, but now, Claire saw them at ease together, dancing on the open floor with dozens of young couples.

Heather's eighth grade passed much like her seventh grade year. Jack was passed into memory, as were Dale and James. The duration of her relationships with boys was a little longer now, but ultimately they went asunder. Usually, she was the one "left", as Heather put it. At the close of her eighth grade year, when James had broken off with Heather, Claire received this letter:

Dear Aunt Claire,

Even though he said it wasn't, I know James hates my hair and my freckles and my braces. I can't wait for next month to get this contraption off my teeth. There's nothing I can do about my freckles and I don't want to dye my hair brown. Susie dyed her hair platinum and it all broke off. She looked like a broom and had to have it cut short like the old pictures you see when boys went to boot camp for the Army. I feel sorry for her. She wears a scarf all the time. Even though I said what I just said about my hair and braces, I know it's more than that, Aunt Claire. What's wrong with me? Every time I get a boyfriend I'm as nice as I can be to him, but he still breaks up with me. What am I doing wrong? James didn't tell the truth a lot, and I always forgave him for that, but he broke up with me anyway. Some of the kids at school have been going steady a whole year. James was my longest boyfriend so far. I wore his ring for 67 days, and I was getting to like him more and more because he said the sweetest things to me. Later I found out he said the same things to Karla when they went steady. I didn't feel as special after she told me that but I still liked him just as much anyway.

Gwen is real popular with the boys so I asked her how to get a boy to like you. She has big blue eyes and blond hair and is really really nice. 'Be kind and happy' is all she said. Aunt Claire, am I kind? I hope I am. I never said a mean word to James, and I never pouted, not once, not even when he said he would call then didn't. Is it always this hard with boys?

Love,
Heather

p.s. I've decided I'm too old to put a little h in my name.

It was July 1st and for Walnut Glen, a mild day. The heat of a California summer was apparent, but not oppressive. There were a few high streaky clouds in the radiant blue sky. Claire even remembered the phase of the moon, a waxing crescent, because the conversation from Heather that day, her fifteenth birthday, surprised Claire.

Early in the morning, Heather had awakened in a somber mood, which was a habit on her birth date every July 1st. Those days were always melancholy for Heather no matter what degree of cheerfulness went on around her.

When Claire had discussed the matter with Rose during one of their luncheons, Rose answered, "She feels abandoned on a subconscious level, in spite of your excellent substitute parenting. In Heather's memory there are no parents. She never knew a mother and father all the years growing up while every child around her had both, or at least one. She feels left out and different. Most young people, and I'm sorry to say many old ones, live in angst if they are not accepted as one of the crowd, and they will do whatever the crowd determines is acceptable in order to belong. Of course, Heather can't bring her parents back from the dead. I find it an interesting paradox that separate people make up a group, yet the overall group takes on a unique demanding personality of its own. It's a terrible pinch on individuality, but it's practiced everywhere, and during adolescence it is especially strong.

"Birthdays are celebrations to commemorate birth. Heather, in a way, was born then deserted. We know she wasn't rejected and that her parents loved her very much, but those are only ideas. You can't touch ideas and hug them and kiss them and they don't smile at you and love you back," Rose finished.

"Will she always feel deserted?"

"Probably."

"Is there a solution?"

"Keep telling her that it wasn't her fault, and she had absolutely nothing to do with it. She has to grasp that life is what it is and we must accept what happens to us because we have no control over the events that uproot our expectations. Advise her about sadness and pain, but also encourage her about the endless possibilities for happiness."

"How do I get her to understand all of that?"

"Tell her!" Rose quipped. "Tell her over and over until you shout it from your dreams. Remember the principle of television and how it pounds at the viewer with its themes. That's what you have to do. Call it brainwashing. You'd be amazed how much sinks in by way of repetition." With her customary twinkling eyes, Rose studied her friend's face, then continued, "I'm going to breech a little confidentiality because I know you will keep the pact of secrecy."

Claire smiled and nodded.

"Many years ago I had a patient who was a young mother of two daughters and had a deep concern for them. She grew up in a family with one other sibling, a sister two years her senior. That sister, for reasons this patient never understood, acted hateful toward her all her life. The older sister's attitude caused a painful burden for this young woman to carry, which is why she came to see me. She had reached out to the sister countless times over the years, but each time she was rejected. Missing the bond and joy of having her sister as a friend, and now with two young girls of her own, she wanted to know how to make them love one another. She was worried they might end up like her and her sister. My answer was the same as I would give you about Heather. Tell them!" Rose chuckled, her smile radiating over the whole of her lean face. "Immediately, that patient began telling each daughter how much she loved the other daughter. Constantly she told both of them, 'You love your sister,' 'You love your sister.' She never gave them a chance to feel or think any other way. And guess what?"

"I think I know."

"Yes. You've never met two sisters that are better friends than those two."

Since that luncheon, Claire worked this idea into her conversations with Heather whenever the timing was right. The loss of Heather's parents had never settled into obscurity. Heather's mother had been a well-loved sister to Claire, and she and Heather reminisced more times than Claire could count about the loving sweetness of Jeanette. She had always wished

Jeanette had gone into nursing or some type of social work because her heart was extra-caring towards others. From Claire, Heather never heard a negative word about her mother, or her father.

Nonetheless, this fifteenth birthday was started as always with a downcast mood when Heather appeared early that morning from her bedroom wearing a soft blue cotton housecoat, her hair disheveled, her feet bare, and glittering pink toenail polish sparkling from her toes. Her teeth had finally been freed from the metal prisons holding them for years. She spent an hour in the bathroom, soaking in the tub, and getting ready for the day. She emerged dressed and groomed. Silently, she proceeded into the kitchen.

Opening the refrigerator, she poured herself a glass of milk then came to sit alongside Claire's large desk, where already Claire had been busy calling for rides so elderly people could get to their doctors' appointments that day. "I've been thinking, Aunt Claire."

Claire laid down her pen and leaned back in her padded leather chair. It squeaked in its regular ways that these two no longer noticed. It would take a fresh observer to regard the bits and pieces of the chair honoring the laws of physics. "I'm fifteen-years-old today," Heather began, as she stared thoughtfully in the direction of the long window near the front door, and out that window into pink and purple cosmos flowers growing with spirited joy in their rich garden soil. "And I've never been to see mom and dads' graves."

She never stood at their deaths. She never loved the ones who loved her completely. She never wandered through the chambers of her heart and believed what was found there. She never walked along silver sands under full moons. She only crabbed in a borrowed shell.

Claire's heart jumped. Heather went forward with her explanation. "For some reason, I never wanted to, Aunt Claire. I figured they were gone forever and what good did visiting a cemetery do anyway? But then I read a true story. It happened in a village in Ireland, and was about a little dog that nobody wanted. It roamed around half-starved until an old man there took pity on it and gave it food every day. When that man died the little dog followed his burial procession to the cemetery. After the man was buried, the little dog stayed and lived on top of the man's grave. If the gardeners chased it away, when they left, the dog would return and fall asleep on the plot again. Even in the harshest winters, the little dog would curl up in the snow and sleep there. Finally, the townspeople decided to help the little animal and built a doghouse for it next to the old man's grave. They brought it food for the rest of its life. When the dog died, they buried it alongside its Master. It was a sad and happy story and started me thinking about cemeteries. Is that strange, Aunt Claire?"

"No, Heather, it's natural to think about cemeteries if you've been reading about cemeteries. What a commendable little dog, and the people who helped him at the end were kind."

Heather took a long drink of milk then placed the glass on a rattan coaster Claire had scattered variously over her desktop for such purpose. With both hands, Heather began smoothing her full red hair toward the back of her head then lifted the entire mass, and with dexterity somehow made a loose knot to hold it aloft. Returning to her milk, she drank deeply, then resumed.

"I've never been to a cemetery and I have two of the most important people in my life buried in one. It suddenly bothered me that I've never so much as visited the graves of my mother and father. But now that I'm thinking about graves, I don't think they would know if I visited them or not, would they, Aunt Claire? I mean, are they somewhere?" Heather waved her arm in an arc to indicate heaven. "Would they even know?"

"I don't think they know about earth any more, nor the people they loved while they were here."

"Then what good would it do to visit their graves?"

"Let me answer that by asking how you think you would feel to visit your parents' final resting places?"

Heather closed her eyes and screwed up her mouth to one side, then opening her eyes she stated, "It makes me afraid."

"Afraid? Why, Heather?"

"Because they're strangers."

"They were your parents. They could never be strangers."

"That's what I mean. I worry that after all these years of hearing about my mom and dad and what special people they were, and looking at their pictures in our scrapbooks, I might get a different feeling at their graves. It's like, you have a heroine and get to thinking she is perfect and you want to be just like her when you grow up. Then one day when you're older, you go to a party, and there she is, but she has dandruff on her shoulders. It spoils the whole thing."

"I've always believed that embracing whatever is true works best."

"But I like the dreamy way of thinking about them."

"Seeing your mom and dad as loving and wonderful isn't 'dreamy', Heather, because they were loving and wonderful people. Their love for you was so great it couldn't be measured."

"I know," Heather answered softly, "That's what you always tell me. But what if something happens there anyway and changes the way I feel?"

"I don't believe that could happen, Heather."

"They were young and beautiful when they had the car wreck, so what if I get a creepy feeling from their graves and they become old and moldy when I think about them?"

"Everyone, even me and even you, become 'old and moldy'. That's the way of all life. Those flowers you've been watching out the window with their color and liveliness will turn brown and wither to the ground and decay."

"I don't like to think about that part."

"You don't have to think about it often, but it's necessary to accept that as a natural process and be at peace with it. For me, when your Uncle Summers, my Oliver, passed away, for a long time I was only able to feel alive when I visited his grave. Even though I don't go as much anymore, when I do, it makes me feel better. It doesn't have anything to do with how someone looked or looks. It's a visit that makes you feel closer to a loved one in your heart. There's something comforting about it. I doubt your dreams would be broken to visit your parents' graves. I think they would be strengthened."

Heather fell silent for several moments, then drained her glass of milk before speaking. "I'll think about it, Aunt Claire." She paused again. "What kind of flowers are those?" She indicated the purple and pink floral display, brilliant now in the glow of the rising sun.

"Cosmos."

"Cosmos," she repeated. Another pause. "I'll think about it, Aunt Claire."

Life proceeded. It was November. Heather was sixteen-years
-old now, having turned that age the past July 1st, and it had
been yet another melancholy birthday for her. It was Wednesday,
and therefore a school day. Heather was a junior in high school
and a growing beauty by all standards.

"My goodness, young lady! You're up early!" Claire paused.
"Is something the matter, Heather?"

Heather turned from her vantage on the couch below the long
front window. She had been staring quietly into the distance, into
a day whose dawn was barely opened. She wore a pair of jeans
and a red sweatshirt. From a side part, her hair fell thick and
curly past her shoulders, and bangs swept in a wave across her
forehead. Her face was somber, almost sad. "Good morning,
Aunt Claire. No, I'm fine. Last night I didn't sleep because I was
thinking about something. Finally, around 3 a.m., I wrote you a
letter. I've been sitting here since then. The letter is on your
desk."

Claire started toward her desk.

"Aunt Claire, please enjoy your coffee first. It's not an
emergency."

"Are you sure?"

Heather nodded her head up and down, but with the same sad
countenance as when Claire had first entered the room. An early
riser all her life, Claire was synchronized to rise with the sun.
She compared that time of day to after a hard rain when sage and
lavender flood the air with fragrant dusky aroma. Typically, no
one is present for these statuesque moments of nature, but if
happened upon, like a vast quiet desert at dawn, a soul's full
attention is seduced. It was these times, at earliest morning, that
Claire captured some of that beauty and did her work in most
flowing ways. But this was the first time in her sixteen plus years
of caring for Heather, except in the infant stages, that her niece
had been awake this early, and with a growing certainty, Claire
suspected some revolution had occurred in her niece. She knew

Heather was not intending to go to school that day because of the way she was dressed.

From the kitchen cupboard, Claire pulled out a gold and red foiled bag with coffee beans inside. Before pushing the button to grind the beans in the electric burr-mill, she started water boiling on the stove, then stole a look into the living room. Heather remained in her motionless posture, staring out the window. Awakening daylight caused her to appear as a silhouette against the window and to take on a back-lighting and glow around her body, like a halo. Claire was not superstitious by nature, but this suggested something ominous to her. In a moment of time, she accepted a unique sanction and approval of whatever incidents lay ahead. She knew they would not issue from darkness.

Claire applied a plastic cone to the top of a glass beaker then settled the ground beans into a paper she had placed inside the cone. She boiled the measured water until it broke into a boil, then slowly poured it over the fresh ground beans. As the water trickled through, coffee aroma filled the kitchen with a sense of comfort and another beckoning day. This is the day the Lord has made. We will rejoice and be glad in it.

Taking her coffee black, Claire picked her favorite porcelain cup, a white container with a shiny 14K band running along its rim. She filled that, and then moved toward her desk. Across the room, Heather hadn't moved. A heavy atmosphere of silence settled over the scene.

Chapter Six

A pink envelope, Heather's usual color choice for stationary, lay on the desk. "Aunt Claire" was written across its blank face in an upright legible handwriting that had refused to be trained into a slant despite Heather's schooling.

Claire especially remembered Heather's sixth grade teacher, a Mr. Hank. He was a tall, military, unfeeling man who had been particularly hard on Heather regarding her handwriting. Heather's natural cursive was straight up and down, proper as a stick, but Mr. Hank demanded she lean her writing to the right. During the whole of Heather's sixth grade year, Mr. Hank summarily returned her reports for rewriting. He was determined to get an angle established in Heather's handwriting because his world was angled. He lived the angle and dreamed the angle. He ate and breathed the angle. We must all write the angle.

Claire knew it was like trying to change Heather's red hair to brown. The long tedious struggles to redo her book reports in a foreign writing style was to Heather an imbroglio she never forgot. Mr. Hank was pleased with the results, oblivious of his deeply negative impact, unaware that all hearts pump their unique song, unaware that his memory would be hard, unfriendly pictures that Heather would carry the remainder of her life. She resumed her natural handwriting after Mr. Hank's sixth grade, and it was this straight vertical-lined lettering that now addressed Claire on the pink paper.

Dear Aunt Claire,

When I became an orphan I was 3 months and 5 days old. I wish my dad wouldn't have wanted that "more for less", as you said he put it, because then he would be here and alive, and so would my mother.

That would be "more" than the "more" he was looking for,

don't you agree? But he didn't make the decision to be happy with less and now he's dead. I don't think such things, at least so drastic, happen to most people when they want "more" in our world and for a long time I have thought it wasn't fair that my mom and dad had to die for that. I think I still feel that way even though we've talked about it so many times and you say life isn't always fair, and that it isn't supposed to be fair, and besides that isn't the point of living. I guess I haven't figured things out yet. I only know I'm kind of mad still, mad at God, mad at life, mad at myself, because if I hadn't been born, my dad probably wouldn't have cared about getting "more".

You said God loves me, but I wonder why Mom and Dad had to die if He loves me. You answered me that God sacrificed even His own Son to pay the punishment for our sins and that's proof of His love. I don't get it. You said justice requires payment for the sins of the world so God gave up his most precious possession to pay and that proves His love for us. Then you said God is perfect and what He does and why He does it are often beyond our understanding. I remember your comparison was that it would be like an ant reading Shakespeare. Okay, but I don't feel right about the car accident yet and for the first time in my life I want to try and do something so I can feel better about being orphaned.

You know how much I love you, Aunt Claire, but you know how a mom and dad loom in a life (I just learned the word "loom" in English from Miss Joyce). Can we go to the cemetery today? I've never been and it's time I went. I've been thinking about it all night. I hope to get some answers and feel better about things, like it's okay that I'm an orphan and that my parents died. Only I'm afraid it will make their deaths too real and it will hurt, but I'm ready to take that chance.

Love, Heather

Ever so slowly, Claire lowered the letter to the desktop. At last! After all the years she had hoped Heather would shut the open breezy door with its chilling winds that had blown against her from the start and chapped her tender heart far too many times. Claire took one slow sip of her coffee then turned her chair around, causing it to voice its customary squawking. Heather hadn't moved from her spot, calmly staring through the flowers out into the awakening world. Occasional cars were beginning to move in each direction in this pleasant east side neighborhood of Walnut Glen.

"Heather, you have made a good decision. I'm proud of you. Once we get there you can spend however much time you like. Okay?"

"Okay," returned a low voice for answer, though Heather hadn't yet stirred.

Finally, they were in the station wagon and on their way. The drive to Walnut Glen Cemetery was about thirty minutes.

Though it was November 7th, the sun and air seemed more in keeping with a June day. This unusual weather, according to the officials, was due to atypical activity in the major wind systems over the planet. El Nino was the name given to the massive weather factory at work in the atmosphere, and it was swirling, plunging, and streaming like a volatile personality. The sun was a summer sun in the month of November. In California, this was not entirely out of character, but on the eastern seaboard, suntan lotions and sunglasses had replaced wool, mufflers, rain gear, and turtle-necked sweaters. Meanwhile, in the Midwestern parts of the United States, snow was falling with a vengeance unheralded in the annals of weather. There, traffic moving home from work was stopped completely all in a row along the roads because of sudden blinding volumes of snow. There was havoc and danger trying to free these motorists, and not all had been saved. Like tantrums, extremes and passions of weather were recorded daily across the country.

At one of their lunches, Rose said the atmospheric elements were like a person, with times of chaos and calm. "Life resembles weather," she said.

Gradually, as though in sympathy with this November summer-like day, Heather warmed to a talkative state. The effervescence of a sixteen-year-old doesn't stay flat for long. "Roy wants to take me to the Homecoming Dance, what do you think?"

"Is Roy the tall lean boy, with light brown curly hair and blue eyes?"

"Yes, that's him, the one with the nice smile."

"I think he's a gentleman. Yes, I think he would be a perfect choice."

"His mother left their family one day. She packed her suitcase and walked out the door leaving Roy's dad, and Roy, and his younger brother. The dad never remarried and none of them ever heard from the mother again. Isn't that horrible?"

"It's unconscionable."

"Aunt Claire! I'm only a junior! What does 'unconscionable' mean?"

"It means shocking and unjust."

"Yes, it is unconscionable," Heather stumbled through the word. "Sometimes Roy and I talk about our mothers being gone. He's easy to talk to. In fact, I've never talked to anyone else about my mother besides you. But with Roy, it's like we both understand what losing a mother means." Heather paused, then wrinkled her brow. "Chuck and Arthur asked me to go with them to the dance too, and I think I have a problem, Aunt Claire."

"Oh?"

"I told all three I would go with them."

"Heather!"

Heather squirmed in her seat. "I didn't want to hurt anyone's feelings."

Claire couldn't help it, she had to chuckle. "I remember doing the same thing in junior high and for the same reason. Eventually I learned how to say 'no', and you will have to learn that too. We can't make everyone happy."

"I just can't say 'no'."

"Yes you can. All you need is practice."

"I've tried, but when I saw Chuck's face all red and embarrassed when he asked me I had to say 'yes'. Besides, I was flattered since lots of girls want to go with him."

"Which boy do you prefer to go with?"

"Roy," Heather answered easily.

"What about Arthur?"

"Arthur is a puffed-up peacock. He's finished with high school and college and has a business of his own in town. It's strange he asked me because he's ten years older than I am. He can still go to our dance as long as his date is a student at the school. But he acts like he thinks he's a gift to the world or something. He came at lunch to the high-school looking for me and had me sort of pinned against my locker when he asked me. In fact, he was squeezing my arm until it almost hurt, so I decided to say 'yes' right away to make him let go of me, which he did, but now I don't know what to do."

"Who is Arthur? I don't remember hearing about him before."

"One of my girlfriends works for him part-time at his video store."

"Does he date younger girls?"

"No. In fact, my girlfriend wanted to date him, but he was only interested in her as an employee, so I was surprised that he paid any attention to me."

Instinctively, some uneasy feeling gnawed within Claire as she listened to the description of this older boy. "Well, you have to decide on one, and tell the others you've made a terrible mistake and apologize to them. But as for Arthur, he needs to know that I don't approve of you dating older boys"

"I'll let Arthur know, Aunt Claire. He's such a snob anyway; but I'm embarrassed to face them."

"It's something you must do."

"I don't know what to say."

"Tell Arthur he's too old for you to date, and let Chuck know you've made other plans and you're sorry. Think about it, Heather. If you had said 'no' to Chuck and Arthur at the beginning they would be over their disappointment by now and Chuck would have asked someone else to go with him. You have to consider what it means for them also. The longer you wait, the harder it will be for Chuck to find a date since most couples have paired off by now. It would have been kinder for everyone if you had said 'no' at the start."

"Either way is hard."

"Doing the right thing is often hard, but it makes you a better person. I know you care about these boys, so telling each one as soon as possible is the most considerate way you can make it up to them."

Heather was silent after this. Their route had become a series of freeway interchanges with loops over and under other road systems. Finally, they reached a single asphalt drive that paralleled the freeway to their left. A tall chain-link fence divided their slow progress from that of the high-speed cars thrusting forward in all their impatient and seemingly imperative destinations.

The road they were on curved right, away from the roar of eternal automobiles, and trucks with spluttering air brakes. Then came a quiet four-lane street, two for each direction, with gray granite buildings set back from the street on grassy knolls. These buildings had always reminded Claire of air-tight banks, except for the large permanent signs on the lawns or over the portals signifying a library or courthouse or high school.

A few blocks later, they saw a sign reading; Walnut Glen Cemetery, with an arrow pointing left. They followed that direction and reached the cemetery entrance within five minutes. Two black wrought-iron gates, its bars made with what resembled long upright pointed spears, were open to allow the passage of automobiles. The only human being visible was one man, the size of a small cat from this distance. He was operating a backhoe and digging what could instantly be surmised was a fresh grave. The cemetery held a cover of shade trees. The gravestones varied according to human notions of art, means, status, love, guilt, or one's particular philosophy of life and death. Heather's parents were buried alongside Claire's husband, Oliver, and though she had never discussed it with Heather, Claire had already purchased her own space next to her husband's. When that unavoidable time arrived, the family would read from left to right: Claire Larsen Summers; Dr. Oliver Winston Summers; Mark Thomas Bainbridge; Jeanette Larsen Bainbridge. There, Claire would return to dust with those she had loved most in life.

"It's lovely, isn't it, Aunt Claire?" Heather noted in a soft voice.

"Yes it is; and peaceful," Claire answered, relieved to hear optimism in Heather's first comment since they had arrived. They traversed several lanes, coming to a stop under the shade of a Birch tree. Though an anomaly in the California climate, it was the largest tree in the cemetery. A slow growing beauty with white papery skin, it was tall and husky. At eye level it forked into two strong branching systems, one of which shaded the area they sought. Claire led the way and soon they were standing before three upright headstones, all in natural mauve stone.

The marker for Claire's husband had the medical staff to represent his profession. Heather's father showed the Shriner's insignia. The last stone, Heather's mother, was etched in a garland of Dogwood tree petals. At times, Claire could hardly believe the living breathing people who had been her most beloved in the world were all departed but for these plots holding their stilled remains.

Heather took Claire's hand in hers and held on with a firm grip. She quietly read her parents' names and dates aloud; first, her father's; then her mother's. "They were so young, weren't they, Aunt Claire?"

"Yes they were, Heather, young and beautiful and good."

Heather continued to study the stones, then finally murmured with a sadness that hurt Claire to hear, "I'll never understand why they were taken from me."

"The reason is a perfect one, whatever it is. The Creator doesn't make mistakes, only people do."

Heather jammed her hands into the front pockets of her jeans. Claire saw tears begin to wiggle down her niece's cheeks, but checked herself from reaching out. This was a personal encounter where Heather needed to connect with reality, a reality denied too long. Sniffing, Heather wiped the tears from her eyes. She looked up to survey the surrounding countryside.

"All I hear are birds," she noted, then sat on the soft warm grass at the foot of her parents' graves, midway between them. Slowly, she reached with both hands and gently placed one on each grave, her left on her father's, the right on her mother's. Heather's head lowered until it came to rest on her chest. From Claire's vantage standing above her, all that was visible was Heather's bundle of red hair, but Claire heard the sniffing and saw the tiny convulsions as Heather wept over these parents she had never known. No one came or went around them, as though this time had been privatized so Heather could release her sorrow, her guilt and confusion, and perhaps leave here with her heart an open sepulcher from which she was finally resurrected, with acceptance that life gives hardships as a natural right.

Some twenty minutes later, the deep quiet storm taking place in Heather's breast abated. She looked up at Claire with red eyes and a pale tear-streaked face. Claire felt an overwhelming compassion for the agony passing through her young niece's and dropped to the ground alongside, taking Heather into her arms and drawing her tightly to herself. "Your parents loved you. You can always know that they loved you."

There was another torrent of convulsing sobs. "They never had a chance to live, Aunt Claire," she squeaked.

"I know, but long life is not what counts. It's what we do with the time we have."

"But we don't know how much time we have."

"No, we don't, so every day is a chance we shouldn't miss to be all we can be."

"My father wanted a bigger house. That's why he died."

Claire knew this was a dangerous subject that could fix a negative impression of her flesh and blood father in Heather's memory. "No, Heather. For the right reasons your father wanted a bigger house for you and your mother. He believed it would make life better for all of you. His intentions were loving and honorable."

"I wonder if they knew, you know, at the last second, I mean. I wonder if their lives flashed by them, the way some people say it does? And maybe they were sorry, or thought they made a mistake or something? Maybe Mom thought the moment before the crash I wouldn't live and neither would they. I wonder so many things about them. Sometimes it hurts to think about it." Heather shook her red mane and looked again at the pastel colored headstones. After a short space of silence, she continued, "Of all the things I wonder about, do you know what I wonder the most?"

"What is that, Heather?"

"I wonder most of all if they are in heaven together and happy." Heather had only just uttered these words when two butterflies, living on late into this unseasonably warm autumn, fluttered by and danced around them. They were medium-sized and of a light yellow color. They were not beautiful specimens to excite a photographer, but they didn't seem to notice or care how they might or might not measure up to some vividly-colored cousin. Rather, they were engaged with one another, as one led, and the other followed one flutter behind in their aerial dance. The soft-winged pair twined over the graves then delicately spun around Heather's head like a halo.

She burst out laughing. "Aunt Claire! The butterflies answered my question!" The instant she spoke, the tiny creatures coasted around her head once more, then puffed away on their papery wings in a path as though they were following tiny invisible mountains and valleys and winding canyons. Heather watched them with a smile until they reached the edge of the cemetery grounds and disappeared over the hedge into the wild grasses of the adjacent meadow.

The following week, from the kitchen Claire heard Heather respond to the front doorbell. There was an exclamation of surprise from Heather, a thank you, then the sound of the front door closing. Within moments Heather appeared, her arms full of long-stemmed red roses.

"My goodness! Who sent you such a lovely gift?"

Sadness passed over Heather's face, "I don't know for sure, but I have an idea."

Together they arranged the aromatic cluster into a tall crystal vase. Claire put clear marbles in the bottom so each rose could be positioned and held in place by the gentle pressure of the marbles as its stem was pushed toward the bottom. The roses were at the stage of beginning to unfurl. Accompanying the roses, were fronds of a delicate fern. These they placed along the outside of the red fountain, and lower than the flower heads, so in appearance the flowers were the crown; the same as they reigned in nature.

The blue envelope that accompanied the bouquet, Heather had laid onto their long rectangular maple table in the sunny alcove off to the side of their spacious kitchen. This is where Claire and Heather took their meals, and where the sun streamed in during the morning hours after first breaking through the white Locust trees looming above that side of the house and perfuming the air with honey scent in early summer.

Claire laid a large round rattan piece at the center of the table, and there Heather placed the floral offering. Both stood back,

Claire with her hands on her hips, and Heather with her hands slipped into the back pockets of her jeans. For several moments neither spoke. Just outside the window, a gentle breeze waved the flowering purple sage growing there with their tall arching boughs, causing the sunlight to break and seem to blink in wonder at the red roses along with Claire and Heather.

Claire broke the silence. "This is from someone who thinks the world of you."

Heather arranged herself in the chair in front of the flowers and reached for the card. The sun was now above the purple sea of sage and fell atop Heather and this red prize, illuminating both as though they were connected.

Claire sat next to her in the armed chair at the table's end, enjoying Heather's profile that showed her distinguished upturned nose. Her curly red locks she had swept to the top of her head and clamped in place there with some kind of a clawed plastic clip that to Claire had an industrial look to it. She had noticed many of today's young ladies using this same hair-piece.

After reading the signature at the bottom of the written message, Heather looked out the window and was quiet. Her freckles were still strong across her nose and along her forearms. Heather complained about her freckles but Claire reminded her that they were natural for a redhead, adding if there were no freckles she wouldn't look normal. Claire's defense of freckles, truly believing they were a human adornment, had never convinced Heather and now in her 16th year, she disliked them more than ever. Her eyes had grown more amber and sparkling as she matured. Insignias of beauty, of parts, of the whole, are assigned deeper than culture with its heave of differences.

Returning her attention to the card, and except for an occasional deep sigh, Heather read silently. Claire enjoyed the beauty of the roses until Heather was ready to reveal the mystery.

Finally, in a low flat voice, she shared, "It's Roy."

"That nice young man! He certainly cares for you!"

"I've made him miserable, Aunt Claire."

"Boys don't usually send flowers unless they're happy and in love."

"Roy isn't like other boys. He's been so kind and good to

me." Heather looked into Claire's face with sadness. "He was always there in a pinch. When I really needed someone, Roy showed up. That's the kind of guy he is."

"Then why is he unhappy?"

Heather looked down at the card again and began to finger it nervously. "He wrote that he understands our talk about me not loving him, and he doesn't want me to feel bad about it. He sent the flowers to cheer me up. Then he adds that his love dies as these flowers die, one by one, and that he will always remember me. Isn't that beautiful, Aunt Claire?"

"It's charming. What an exceptional young man. Your average boy would bully you to love him, then get angry and turn with a snort if you didn't and act like he didn't care anyway. Roy sounds as though he can genuinely love. But he sounds melancholy for such a young man."

"It's because of his mother. When she deserted their family he was only three-years-old. The father did a good job raising Roy and his brother, but there's a deep wound that Roy feels because his mother deserted them. It's sort of like me, Aunt Claire, but in another way. We both were orphaned young. Maybe that's why he likes me so much. Plus, he's loyal and doesn't look at other girls when we're together."

"It sounds as though he loves you for who you are."

"But I don't love him back and that's the problem."

"Oh?"

"I mean, I like him a lot, and I even sort of love him, but not the way he loves me. I'm not ready to settle down yet because I could never go steady with Roy and go everywhere just with him. I don't know how to explain it, Aunt Claire. It's like you can't make yourself love someone."

"You're right, Heather, not even if Roy is the nicest person under heaven. That's been a mystery since the beginning of time and caused more books to be written and poems to be penned and songs to be composed than any other subject in the world. It's something that happens between a man and a woman, or it doesn't, and often there isn't any logic to it."

"I'm glad I didn't live in a time or place when parents did the choosing for their children."

"The odd thing, Heather, is that those marriages usually

ended up as good or better than the ones we have in America."

Heather stared at her aunt. "How is that possible?"

"It must be a state of mind, with total submission to the parents' wishes. No one thinks to question what he or she has always been taught is the correct way to arrive at marriage, so it goes smoothly when the time comes. Studies of those marriages show that if there were no sparks at the start, love grows and the marriage often becomes tender and caring."

"I would rather take my chances."

"So would I. Then again, I look at the divorce rates in our country at fifty percent and wonder if the ancient way might be best after all."

"It's not right," Heather complained, "to have nothing to say about the one person you marry and spend the rest of your life with."

"Yes, the idea is appalling, and I love freedom as much as you, but on a different level, freedom can loose hateful behavior in humans, as though wicked personalities are waiting inside for any chance to escape. It's shocking to read ancient records and learn how human beings have treated one another. I'm not talking about choosing a mate and marriage now; I'm talking about our overall humanity. It's hard to accept the cruelty we've perpetrated onto one another." Claire realized she had taken another direction, but she also knew her mind wanted to go this way. Heather stopped tracing one of the swirls on an opening rosebud with her finger, and cupped her hands together on the maple surface of the table. She turned her amber eyes toward her aunt. "Can you give me an example, Aunt Claire?"

Claire hesitated because she didn't know if at sixteen years of age a young woman should hear such things and she knew once you see, once you hear, once you experience, there's no erasing it. But she decided one aspect of wisdom is knowledge, so she answered.

"Every Age has cruelty, Heather. Other than dying from natural causes, danger from other humans has always been greater than threats from floods or famine or disease. One great philosopher named Sartre, said, 'Hell is people.' It's shuddering to think how once thousands of people would attend an event, the way we go to a football game, to watch people slaughter people."

"When was that?"

Again, Claire fell silent, following the line of thought how modern people in essence still participate in the Coliseum of Rome, but instead of live murders, they watch simulated attacks and murders on television and movie screens. The blood and gore are ever present. She shook off the image and responded.

"In the Coliseum of Rome, Gladiators fought to the death to please the cheering crowd. The Emperor and Empress were given the best seats to watch the death struggle and most of Rome, young and old ate iced refreshments as they witnessed the battle until death. It was like going to a movie or a play. A good seat at the Coliseum was prized."

"You mean they weren't sickened?"

"No."

We are schizophrenic. The negative self drinks blood and breathes it in like a sweet scent. These lurkings are from darkness, and such cravings are real. Things are done that don't follow God's arrangement, but Free Will gives permission to spit in your mother's face.

"How could anyone watch that and cheer for it?"

"There is wickedness buried in every human heart, Heather, but many people throughout time won't admit that about themselves or others."

"Is my heart wicked?"

"Yes, and so is mine."

"My heart doesn't feel wicked."

"It is, Heather. It's in us the moment we are conceived. That doesn't mean kindness and compassion are missing, nor love, virtue, or faith. All of that is also who we are."

"I don't know how anyone could be bad enough to enjoy murder. That's sickening."

"What's sickening is that so many people were comfortable with it. There was open acceptance. It was considered a normal, every-day event."

"Is that where Christians were fed to the tigers and lions?"

"By the thousands."

Heather shuddered.

"I'll tell you one more story, and then we'll talk about something more pleasant." Claire paused. "Other times in our history torture was used. Some legal prosecutors of antiquity would get their confessions any way they could. Oliver's father was an attorney and studied both law and its history. He shared with us that historically, torture devices were commonly used on the accused, but one instrument in particular disturbed him. It was a metal device, shaped like an egg that fit around the human skull. A screw was turned a little each day in order to gradually crush the skull."

"No!"

"Yes, that's bad, but worse was that the mechanism had a comfortable platform build onto it where the man who operated the machine could sit and relax or daydream or do whatever someone did then to pass the time of day. Occasionally, he would lean down to hear the moans, and hopefully the confessions of his victims."

How contrasted this sunny well-furnished kitchen alcove, with its brilliant red roses signifying love was, to lives in some remote chamber ages ago where skulls were slowly crushed.

"I could never have watched any of it!" declared Heather.

"Many young women like you considered it as nothing more than a regular day to attend the Coliseum."

"Then it depends on your culture as to whether you accept or hate cruelty?"

"To a large degree, yes. Good and evil have repeatedly conquered and re-conquered one another from the beginning of human existence."

"Nobody knows better during the evil times?"

"Only some."

Heather was silent awhile before speaking, "Will it stop some day?"

"The human heart doesn't change, only the circumstances surrounding it do. The danger is with us and within us for all time. There is an old American Indian proverb that talks about the good wolf inside and the bad wolf inside, and how the person will become which of these he or she feeds."

"I don't want to be cruel," Heather answered, gazing at the flowers, "And I feel as though I have been. When I told Chuck I couldn't go to the Homecoming Dance with him, his face turned crimson. He gets embarrassed real easy. The other girls think it's cute, but I feel sorry for him." Heather tapped her thumbs together, "He shook his head up and down to show me he understood then walked away without a word.

"When I told Roy I wasn't going with him he stared at me for a long time then leaned over and kissed me on the top of my head. I'll never forget the sadness on his face.

"I've hurt their feelings. Should I write them a letter too, and apologize?"

"I think that's a good idea. But I'm confused." She pointed to the flowers. "You told Roy 'no', you told Chuck 'no', so who is it you're going with to the Homecoming Dance?"

"Arthur," Heather answered.

"The older boy you called a 'peacock'?"

Heather giggled. "Yes, him!"

"What changed your mind about Roy?"

"Arthur."

"You know I'm not happy with that, Heather."

"I know, Aunt Claire, but you'll understand once I tell you what happened.

"I went to Arthur first to tell him I was going with Roy. He said I was not going with Roy, I was going with him. His eyes almost burned a hole through me when he said it. His body was stiff and he stepped so close I could feel the warmth of his breath on my face." Heather giggled.

Claire gave her a perplexed look.

"It was so cute, Aunt Claire. As soon as he got that close everything changed. He went sort of limp. He took both my hands and his were trembling! I'm not sure, but I think his lower lip was quivering too, and he said 'Please?' in the softest, kindest, sweetest voice I've ever heard. It was impossible to say 'no'!" Heather laughed again. "My girlfriends think I'm crazy not to go with Chuck, but Arthur was too adorable the way he said 'Please?' that I just have to go with him!" Claire studied the happiness on Heather's face, debating whether or not to say anything more. Her better judgment caused her to speak. "It worries me, Heather, because Arthur is ten years older than you. He's more experienced in life and that could mean you get hurt in the end."

"Oh, Aunt Claire, it's fine. He's a really nice guy. If you had heard him say "Please?" the way he did, you would understand why I said 'yes'." Another giggle sprang from her.

Reluctantly, Claire would allow this, but she would watch over it like an accountant fidgeting with his numbers. She added, "Just for fun, let's pretend we were living long ago in an eastern culture and I was the parent making the choice for you. Which boy do you suppose I would select for you?"

Heather pressed her lips together tightly and studied the ceiling as she contemplated the answer. "Chuck!" she exclaimed.

Claire pointed to the roses.

"Roy?"

"Yes, and now I'll fix breakfast. How about French toast?"

"Uh huh," Heather answered absentmindedly, keeping her eyes on the roses as Claire moved inward to the working part of the kitchen.

Chapter Seven

Claire found a message next to her coffeemaker the following morning.

Dear Aunt Claire,

I wrote to Chuck and here it is for you to see before I give it to him. May I have your opinion first? The roses are dying. Every day I pull another one out from the rest. Only seven are left. As they die, I keep remembering Roy. Anyway, here's Chuck's letter:

Claire pulled a pink scented sheet from its pink envelope and first scanned the neatly written handwriting in its upright vertical style, noticing that Heather's capital letters had taken on a swirling construction of loops and sweeping tails. Her letter ran thus:

Chuck,

You were so sweet to invite me to the Homecoming Dance. I'm sorry I disappointed you. We're both 16 years old and I've been told at this age we'll still have lots of boyfriends and girlfriends before we settle down with one person. Gail told me she's crazy about you and would love for you to ask her to the dance. You could double date with her twin sister and her date. You're a real nice guy. I'll see you at the dance. Maybe we can dance one dance together?

Your friend,
Heather Bainbridge

Her letter to Roy was along these same lines.
The letters will help these boys, Claire thought, but their

youth will help them more. The end of the world for a teenager quickly becomes a bright tomorrow.

A few days before the dance a chill settled over Walnut Glen. The month of November had returned to its expected cloudy rainy days, with sun peeking through occasionally as if to see how things were going on the surface of the planet, before sheltering behind more clouds and showering the earth again with rain and cold. These were the first rains of the season, and welcome in that regard. There was also the feeling of a cusp in the atmosphere, something high and unsettling, something tight and cool about the weather. It seemed to circle above as it explored the land below for its winter nest, as though it had migrated to reach this place. There was no longer any doubt that winter was marshaling and as in this trickle, or suddenly, it would take dominion. How utterly helpless man is before the monarchy of weather.

Cold winds loosed the remaining yellow, orange, brown and red leaves from the trees, and the various wind chimes in Claire's garden were heard to tremble and melody the air. Her favorite, a glass-hooped arrangement with the glass tempered to withstand 35 mile-an-hour winds, hung just outside the front door, sheltered from the harshest weather. The tinkling cymbals of glass hitting glass brought to mind a boat trip she and Oliver had taken once, to a grotto in Europe. In their canoe, the squeeze into the cave was like traveling through a birth canal. Their guide had deftly handled the tight passage until they emerged inside, onto a quiet placid pool of water undisturbed by the pounding surf outside. The ceiling was high-roofed. Sounds echoed sweetly in this watery womb as the guide rowed around the large pool. It was reversing troubles each soul endures, for a place where angels live and sing. Water dropping off the ends of the oars dripped loudly as though amplified ten thousand times. It appealed deeply and memorably to Claire. Since that time, she thought one hadn't truly heard the cymbals of water until one visited a grotto by the sea.

Heather was glamorous the night of the Homecoming Dance. She had gathered her hair at the back of her neck with a large

71

black velvet bow. From that restriction, it gradually fanned outward into a thick wavy garden of red that nearly reached her waist. After reading about ladies in other countries wearing glowing or blinking bugs in their hair when going out at night, Heather had purchased some tiny silver glitter stars and sprinkled them lightly into her hair. The subtle twinkling was becoming, and Claire knew it would be even more so under the faceted glass ball at the dance that evening.

She wore a full-length black velvet dress, scooped in the back. It was sleeveless and cut inward and angular in the bodice then upward where it became a high neck, like a soft black collar. She wore long black gloves and her black heels were silk. A crystal necklace with its layers leading to a large faceted crystal hanging from the center, and with bracelet and earrings to match, stunned even Claire with Heather's youthful beauty presented so womanly.

Stiffly, Heather paced around the living room, peering out the curtains along the front window every few seconds for a sign of Arthur's black long-finned car. She had closed and arranged the floral crepe floor-length curtains with their opaque sun-blocking lining in such a way that she could peek out undetected.

While Heather nervously moved, Claire was busy at her desk arranging tomorrow's relief for an elderly husband and wife. The husband had suffered a fall and needed help to get into and out of bed for many weeks to come. His little wife had grasped Claire's hand that morning at the hospital. That one gesture, with no words exchanged, told Claire how grateful and perhaps desperate they were.

"He's here!" Heather blurted, and moved quickly past Claire to the hallway, then down that wooden way to her room, behind which she now disappeared, calling before she closed the door, "Please answer the door, Aunt Claire, then come and get me!"

Heather had a knack for timing entrances and this one had been carefully planned. The doorbell rang with repeated pushing on the button as though the visitor believed the people inside might be in a far off room, or nearly deaf. Either that, Claire thought, or this bold young man wants the world to know he is an important event that has arrived.

Opening the door, Claire looked into several dozen long-stemmed yellow roses, which moved slightly to the left, exposing the face of Arthur Conway. Claire had only seen him from a distance when he dropped Heather off at the curb after school. He was a handsome youth, with swarthy skin and black wavy hair. His eyes were brown, and had a pleading look to them. His ears were slightly large, but tempered by the ample dark waves of hair streaming back along the sides of his head. His mouth was small, full, and nicely shaped. The one poor feature was his nose. It was slightly thick and classic Greek aquiline in profile. But taken all together, Arthur was a handsome young man, in spite of what Claire thought was a snarl upon his lips. She wasn't certain if this was nature's doing or if Arthur had assumed the posture in some notion of the personality he wished to present to the world.

"How do you do, Arthur, I'm Heather's aunt, Claire Summers."

The roses jiggled as Arthur re-arranged his hold on the flowers in order to free his right hand. Claire was met by a gripping handshake that caused pain to shoot through her knuckles. She suppressed a wince.

"Yeah Hi, I'm Arthur Conway, nice to meet you." His voice was high-pitched and rapid. "Heather has told me about you, how you've raised her. I know about her mom and dad. May I come in?" he added in the same breath.

Claire stepped aside and swept her left arm inward. "Please do."

Arthur strode by, his lanky frame clothed in a black tuxedo with tails. As he did so, Claire experienced a wave of inexplicable words that formed in her mind, repeating, "It won't work. It won't work."

"Would you like to sit down?"

"No thanks. I'll wait here."

"I'll get Heather," Claire offered, and left Arthur standing in the middle of the living room taking stock of his surroundings.

Heather was suppressing a giggle with her hand when Claire entered the bedroom. She was radiant. "Aunt Claire! Did you see the car?"

"What car?"

"The limousine!"

"Limousine?"

"Look!" She took Claire's hand and led her to the window at the opposite end of her spacious bedroom. Heather drew aside her pink floral curtains, and Claire saw a long white limousine by the curb outside. "Isn't he wonderful?" Heather squealed. She cleared her throat working to gain composure, then solemnly announced, "I'm ready."

She hesitated in the middle of her room, facing the bedroom door. First she wiggled her shoulders then shook her arms as though loosening her body to become relaxed. She straightened her back, paused a moment, then ushered from the room as though facing her court, her destiny, or her doom, Claire wasn't sure which.

She decided to linger a while in Heather's room to give the young couple time to greet and admire one another until their nervousness was dispelled. Meanwhile, Claire still wondered if Arthur had been tense or if that handshake was his normal grip.

According to Heather the dance was perfect. For days she was effervescent, then bundles of flowers began to arrive each week: Gerbera daisies; Peruvian lilies; gladiolas in spikes of fat bright buds on the verge of unfurling into magnificent plumage; roses, at times long stemmed and large of flower, at other times delicate and in blushing bud; but mainly orchids by the dozens. In a stream they came, these treasures of nature, and with each arrival Heather's amber eyes shone with what Claire knew was a gathering love. Every afternoon after school, the sleek black car pulled to a stop at the curb, and Heather spilled out, usually laughing, her red hair like a flame under the sun to match her leaping spirits. At home, she sang, she hummed, Claire even saw her twirling in the living room once as she awaited Arthur's honk to drive her to school in the mornings, her full skirt like an ecliptic plane of blue below which two ivory legs of fine shape galloped her in circles.

Dear Aunt Claire,

I'm in love! I never thought it would happen but then there never was an Arthur before. He is so sweet to me. I feel like I've known him forever. We've been together almost two years. I can't remember how it was before him. I love being in love. It's hard to believe I'm through with high school and will be starting nursing school in a few months. My birthday is next week. I'm going to be 18 years old on July 1st, and Arthur said he has something special for me. He already gives me so many things I can't think of what's left. Aunt Claire, do you think this is the way my mom and dad felt about each other? Is this the way you felt toward Uncle Oliver? I always thought love...real love...was a nice idea but I didn't know it felt like this. I count the minutes when I'm away from Arthur, and every time I see him I'm so happy. He is the whole world to me. I think he sleeps under my pillow because I dream about him all night long. I can't describe how happy I am!

Love,
Heather

p.s. How does Heather Bainbridge Conway sound? Just kidding!

On July 1st, Heather was up at dawn. She had swept her hair into a cluster atop her head and pinned some small yellow roses from Arthur's most recent bouquet into the curls. Her dress was white cotton with a large orange floral pattern of peonies on it. There were shoulder straps and the skirt was to mid-calf. She wore her favorite necklace, given to her by Arthur, a faceted red garnet piece that was one continuous loop of the gemstones tied in such a way as to form a succession of little flowers in appearance along the length of the long circular strand. It glittered with a thousand facets whether in the sun or not. All one needed was lack of utter darkness to bring alive the endless hours of labor from an obscure gem cutter in India who probably could never afford the necklace over which he or she had toiled so long. But these thoughts were as far from Heather as the east is from the west. Love is all consuming when it is new. For shoes, she wore yellow leather sandals with a loop around the great toe. They slapped slightly against her heels as she walked.

Claire had awakened that morning to Heather coming through

the bedroom door with a tray containing a mug of steaming coffee. "Don't get up, Aunt Claire. I've done everything I can think to do waiting for 9 a.m. and Arthur to get here, so I made you a Cappuccino. You enjoy it. Don't hurry. I'll go back to the window and wait."

"Happy Birthday," Claire offered, from her pillow.

"Thank you," Heather whispered, then carefully laid the tray next to Claire on the oak table alongside the bed before slipping out of the room.

Claire was aware of a veritable blur of colors, along with a lingering trail of perfume that she recognized as Christian Dior. It was the only perfume Arthur wanted Heather to wear, and he made sure she had it in constant supply.

One yellow rose had been removed from the recent dozens Arthur had sent and this Heather had placed into a sterling silver vase designed for a single flower. Arthur gave the vase to Heather at the beginning of their relationship with instructions that she was always to keep one fresh flower from his offerings in that vase at her bedside so he would stay in her thoughts. Happily, Heather had complied and Claire knew it was an offering Heather now made on this morning platter to share her overflowing heart, by joining the vase holding its one fresh flower with Claire's morning ritual of coffee.

Arthur was Heather's Eucharist. He was her Sacraments, the Body and the Blood, her Covenant, her Salvation. He was her Bread of Heaven, her Manna, her King and Lord of All. He was her Confessional and the place she went for all things under the sun.

Finished with her coffee, Claire wrapped in her purple cotton housecoat and carried her tray toward the kitchen.

Heather was standing in the living room in front of the long window looking out, humming and swaying. She kept her eyes toward the street as she fingered her garnet necklace.

At exactly 9 a.m., a black limousine stopped at the curb. Arthur emerged after the driver walked around the car and opened his door.

He stood tall, looking right and left down either direction along Heather's block, as though enjoying the morning view, or relishing the attention the limousine caused from the various residents already stirring in this warm day. He was outfitted as though for a gentleman's safari. The prey was a young girl whose heart he knew beat for him alone. Here, the grass was not tall. Here, there were no sudden leaps of growling and fangs and talon claws. Here, cubs rolled in playful safety on the plains.

His shirt and long shorts were Khaki cotton, and his sandals were black leather. For adornment, even from here, his heavy gold chains were noticeable; one on his wrist, and two around his neck. Though some males were beginning to pierce their ears, Arthur called it "sissy" and had rejected the idea. Heather told Claire about Arthur's feelings on this subject. She shared it as though it was a revelation, as though it was God's truth. No matter which way the straying children of Israel wandered, Arthur was the Oracle. Forty years! Forty years! All Arthur's doing. He was omniscient.

From the kitchen, Claire watched Heather as Arthur began his approach to the front door. No longer did she hum and sway. No longer did she finger her red garnet necklace. She had transported into stillness. Her entire attention was on the young man approaching the rows of cosmos once more in bloom, as was their want. These rich bountiful flowers had no option but to follow their inner composing, and this year as every year, in perennial glory they came forth with what could only be described as a type of joy. Enthusiastically, they were all they could be. Like Heather, they were in love. Their lover was the sun and the water and the good great earth.

Heather spun around to face Claire, her face beaming. "Aunt Claire! A Limo! Isn't he wonderful?"

Before Claire could answer, Heather had hurried to the door at the first rap of Arthur's knocking. He stood, with a bouquet of yellow orchids. Down the center of each petal there was a wide red strip and from that line red specks were sown like freckles onto the remaining yellow surface. Heather clutched them to her bosom.

Leaning over, Arthur sought Heather's lips, and they met in a prolonged kiss above the flowered love offering. When they parted, still with their faces close and looking deeply into one another's eyes, Arthur called her "Turtle" then added, "I love you. Happy birthday."

Claire had slipped out of sight in order to give them privacy, even though she doubted they were aware of her presence. She heard low murmuring, occasional light laughter, and the word, "Turtle" float affectionately above the general sounds of these young lovers.

Heather swept into the kitchen, as Arthur followed behind her canceling with playfulness Heather's comments that the orchids were extravagant. "Not when they're for you, Turtle."

"But they're too expensive," she continued to tease.

Arthur answered suddenly and hard, "No they aren't!"

Heather turned to face him from the sink area, where after dressing Claire had joined her to help snip the bottom of the stems in an angular cut to allow a greater surface for water absorption.

Arthur's face was set in a firm way, his eyebrows drawn together. "Because you're worth it, plus, you can always have the memory of these flowers, so it isn't money wasted."

"Why, yes, that's true," Heather returned gaily, "And I will remember them, Arthur. They're beautiful." She gently cupped several blossoms and leaned into them, her eyes closed. She inhaled deeply then made a delightful moan. Looking up, she smiled at Arthur.

He nodded back to her stoically, but with obvious pride in her pleasure.

The flowers were set in the kitchen alcove atop a coaster on the long maple table. Claire momentarily recalled a vase of red roses that had once stood there, roses from a promising boy named Roy, a boy Claire felt certain would leave a good and decent mark in life.

While Heather fluttered to and from her bedroom, Arthur stood stiffly in the center of the living room noticeably enjoying Heather's last preparations to leave with him on this, her 18th birthday. She leaned over to Claire on one of those passes and whispered, "He still hasn't said what the surprise is."

"You mean it's not the Limousine and orchids?" Claire whispered back.

"No, it's something else. He says it's so special I'll have to sit down when he tells me!" Claire felt uneasy. There was no underpinning of words, but Claire instinctively felt that something disturbing was about to happen.

"Two minutes!" Heather called and disappeared the final time into her room for an umbrella against the glaring sun. With red hair and a fair complexion, she had learned to brave the stares from people as she carried an umbrella in the months of July and August to protect herself from the burning rays.

Once, her delicate skin had burned so badly her skin blistered and she laid in bed agonizing for days. When her doctor suggested she carry an umbrella like people in eastern cultures where the sun shines intensely hot, Heather took to the idea. Not one to go against customs, it was bold behavior for her. She and Claire had talked about what it meant to carry an umbrella in America during the summer. They knew it would subject Heather to odd reactions even though it is considered normal and expected in other sunny lands of earth. In spite of drawing attention, Heather decided in favor of it. At first her girlfriends said she looked silly and had no sympathy for Heather's fair skin and vulnerability to the sun's ultraviolet rays. They were more concerned about getting all the sun they could on their skin in order to show a tan. Heather tried to tell them she didn't tan, she only burned, but they didn't listen so she gave up defending herself and let them think whatever they wanted.

Claire had congratulated her on good common sense and health safety. She was impressed by Heather's choice of a strikingly feminine white-laced parasol with a scalloped edge and a white satin ribbon threaded through the eyelet border. Yet even in her conviction, Heather had at first handled the covering furtively, trying whenever possible to duck into shade so she could close the white shield. But over time and with the ease that comes with habit, she was no longer self-conscious about her parasol, or the reactions of the public.

"Where are you taking Heather for her birthday, Arthur?" Claire approached him as he stood, fingering what was now a full dark moustache drooping around the outer edges of his mouth.

Arthur turned his attention onto her then spoke with a crisp tone that always managed to confuse Claire because his warm-looking brown eyes invited, but the tenor of his voice rebuked. "I'm taking her somewhere she's never been," he answered evasively.

"Is it a secret, or might I know where that is?" Claire's tone was slightly challenging.

"Sorry," he answered in his high-pitched way, "she has to be the first to know. Don't worry, she's in good hands and I'll have her back by the time the sun goes down." He pat Claire's arm with a clumsy swat meant to console her.

Heather came into the living room, carrying her parasol by its strap on her wrist.

As the limousine pulled away from the curb with its young cargo in the back seat, Claire waved, then realized they hadn't noticed her because they were face to face in love.

For the rest of the day there was an underlying anxiety Claire felt about Arthur's intentions, and whatever his big secret was. Clearly, she knew there was a conflict, though she kept it quietly to herself, regarding how different her feelings were about Arthur compared to Heather's total capitulation of heart mind and soul toward him. Paramount to Claire was Heather's happiness, so she didn't understand why she felt these reservations since the signs of Arthur loving Heather were constant. True, he was ten years her senior, but Rose had put her mind somewhat at ease regarding the age discrepancy at one of their luncheons.

"The years don't matter," she had said, "but intentions do."

"Do you think he's smitten with her youth and vulnerability?"

"Maybe yes, maybe no, but not all men are deceivers. His motives could be honorable, but watch carefully that he doesn't show signs of manipulation, like encouraging Heather how to dress and what jewelry to wear and how to walk and what to say and those types of things. That would suggest he intends to control her."

Claire had watched for over two years, and unfailingly Arthur was attentive and dependable. He showered Heather with gifts and he made her happy. Finally, Claire had conceded that Arthur could be an authentic lover. She wished, however, that this nagging little voice inside with inaudible rejecting feelings toward Arthur would either stop or make itself comprehensible.

She got through this day by sinking into the needs of others. In fact, most of her afternoon was taken up quite forgetful of Heather and Arthur, as she assisted an elderly and sweetly smiling lady into the passenger seat of her station wagon, then to a doctor's appointment. Betty was the widow's name, and Claire knew she was 88-years-old. Still ambulatory, Betty managed slowly and competently around her apartment. But she was a forgotten woman, without family, and at times in need of transportation. Claire had developed a friendship with her, so Betty now felt comfortable calling Claire for help to get her somewhere important. Claire was delighted to oblige. Betty's beaming face and delicate weak voice were ample rewards.

When Claire returned home around 3 p.m., she was surprised to find Heather already home, sitting alone and motionless on the couch, staring out through the floating cosmos and into the distance. Claire knew in an instant that Heather saw no further than her heart.

Checking her concern, she spoke as casually as her voice would allow. "Hello, Heather, I didn't expect you so soon."

Heather answered in a monotonous tone, "I asked Arthur to bring me home." Her preoccupation was like a spell.

This was too much for Claire and immediately she moved to Heather's side, lowering her face to be on a level with Heather's profile. "What's happened?"

Heather fingered her garnet necklace with her right hand, rubbing the small faceted gems unconsciously. Her lips began to work in twisting movements, preparing to switch her thoughts into language. "He's serious, Aunt Claire. I sort of knew, but..." she didn't finish.

"Look at me, Heather. Tell me what's going on between you and Arthur."

Slowly, Heather turned her attention onto Claire's face. Claire had never before seen Heather so serene or womanly.

"He wants to marry me. We're engaged." Heather lifted her left hand and displayed a dazzling diamond ring, set in Tiffany style. It was the largest diamond Claire had ever seen. Four large rectangular diamonds, two on each side, and cut in emerald design; baguettes, Heather called them, were set along the band below the towering diamond.

For a split second, followed instantly by self-chastisement, Claire saw the sad elderly people she knew who were struggling on small pensions and doing without. One needed a wheelchair, another could use a hospital bed, and a young father of three lacked the funds for a liver transplant. Claire shook these thoughts away. This was Heather's moment, her once in a lifetime experience to be proposed to by the man she loved.

But Claire was less than thrilled. She knew her thoughts and feelings and duty regarding Heather. She looked into Heather's eyes. Her heart felt sad and heavy. "Heather, I am being honest with you when I say I'm not sure Arthur is the right man for you."

Heather's eyes opened wide. "He loves me and I love him, Aunt Claire!"

"Many times people have loved each other, even though they weren't a good match."

Heather stared, speechless, at her aunt.

"I worry that Arthur will make the decisions about your life and by doing that you will never develop your natural potential." Claire hesitated, not sure if she should continue, but she knew this was the time to express her doubts. "I'm also concerned about Arthur's extravagant spending. In your future, there could be real trouble because of it.

"Heather, I love you, and I encourage you to think about your dream of becoming a nurse. Are you willing to give up that dream, or would Arthur encourage you to attend nursing school, perhaps part-time?" Claire decided that was enough said; and probably too much.

There was a profound silence as Claire and Heather looked at each other. Claire waited for Heather to speak.

"It was outer silence, but loud declaring within. Sirens came together screaming, 'Me! Me! Choose Me!'"

"I love you Aunt Claire, but Arthur is the most important dream of my life." She smoothed her white and orange peony floral dress and began swiveling her engagement ring left and right. "Isn't it the most beautiful thing you've ever seen? Arthur won't tell me how much he paid for it, but he hinted it was over $20,000.00. I can't believe he actually wants to marry me. I can't believe he loves me this much." Heather indicated the diamond ring again, spreading her fingers and admiring its dazzling triumph to pull all eyes to itself.

Claire knew Arthur had Heather's heart, live and pumping in

his open hands. She knew she could not demand Heather give up Arthur. To do so would cause them to want to be together even more. She tapped Heather's engagement ring.

"I've never seen one more lovely. The video business must be booming."

"Arthur has added two stores and his are the busiest in town. Now he's talking about opening more in neighboring towns. He's a genius at business. He's so smart. He said we can work together in the stores. He'll teach me how to do the books and run the cash register and things like that."

An image of Heather on a raised platform behind a cash register renting movies to all walks of life was a horrid contrast to the altruism Claire knew lay fertile in Heather's heart. "Then you're giving up your plans to become a nurse?"

"Arthur says life is that way. You can't know what's in the future, and now that we have each other, my life will join his and we'll work together to make our living."

"How do you feel about that, Heather?"

"Arthur says a woman is to respect and obey her husband." Heather turned to face Claire. "Is that true, Aunt Claire?"

"It works both ways. Arthur must respect your wishes too. The truest love means caring most about what is best for the other person. Both husband and wife should live this way toward each other."

"I want to do everything I can to make Arthur happy."

"And so must he want that for you. Can you be happy giving up your dream of nursing to work in a video store?"

"If I'm with Arthur, I'll be happy anywhere, as long as we're together."

Claire recognized this young beautiful vibrant niece of hers was in the net of love and nothing was in there with her but Arthur. If Heather would ever emerge from that fibrous hold; if she would ever develop her inner self; Claire couldn't know. Yet at bottom, something gnawed at her, something unhappy and fearful for Heather. "Have you talked about a wedding date?"

"My birthday next year. I'll be 19, and..." Heather stopped and smiled shyly. A red flush covered her face. "Arthur says I'll be harvest ripe by then." She glanced at Claire, "He's such a tease. Sometimes I get sort of nervous the way he watches me, like he's studying me or something."

"He's admiring you. After all, you are a beautiful young woman and his betrothed. He's enjoying thinking that all his life he will have you as his wife." To herself, Claire added, "At least I hope that's what he's thinking." She embraced Heather. "I'm happy for you," but Heather's expression was sober when they separated.

"Do you think I'm too young to get married?"

"Yes."

Heather's eyes widened. "But you just told me you were happy for me, Aunt Claire!"

"I am."

"But you say I'm too young?"

"Yes I do."

Heather's brows knit together as she continued searching Claire's face. "Do you think I should say 'no'?"

Claire knew this was the foundational cement of a relationship that would build and stand, or build and crumble, and she wanted to be there with Heather if the goings were smooth or if the goings were rough. Carefully, she warmed to the answer that would always be remembered by Heather at this critical choice of paths in her life; but she had to be honest. "You're young, Heather, and you haven't dated any boys besides Arthur since you were a junior in high school. You have no way to compare him to other boys you may care for as much or even more than Arthur. I think you should go out with other boys and be less serious with Arthur until you are older and have more experience. If you do this for a few years then decide you love only Arthur, there is still no urgency to be married. You could date during nursing school and when you have your license, then, perhaps you could talk about marriage."

Claire hesitated, glancing out into the warm summer day. Cars were moving by, each about its necessities or wants. She was grieved by, suddenly engulfed by, an awareness of wasted time, of wasted opportunities, of wasted lives frittered away on valueless expeditions that often seemed utmost in importance to the understanding, yet were senseless, even cruel wastes of life.

She faced Heather again. "My strongest advice for you is to wait."

"Oh, Aunt Claire! I know this is true love I feel for Arthur and we want to be together. Please try and understand." Heather leaned over, embraced Claire, and said, "I love you," then sprang from the couch and rushed into her room. In moments, Claire heard her voice. The distance muffled the words, but its tone was clearly understood. Heather was elated and sharing her marital acceptance with who could be none other than Arthur Conway.

Claire felt defeated and utterly responsible for this outcome. She reprimanded herself for allowing Heather to date this boy from the start, and not giving input to guide it from becoming serious. She sighed deeply, with a gush of air, and muttered, "Well, Jeanette, dear sister, maybe I didn't do such a good job raising your Heather after all, and now she is a young woman making her own decisions. I hope you would approve of this man she has chosen. I know Mark wouldn't; and neither do I."

She rose and started toward the kitchen to prepare dinner before she began the paperwork awaiting her which addressed the needs of others as they lay stacked as words on pieces of papers arranged in neat piles atop her desk. Flesh and blood and beating hearts with souls and wrong choices and bad luck and every assortment of trouble, who had finally in their desperation reached out for help. Claire felt her greatest gift in life was to be able to reach back and in some small way help those who were suffering.

Chapter Eight

The world continued to spin and move its cosmic ways. Heather was a copper blur and seldom without the slender dark-complexioned, black-haired Arthur alongside in their busy comings and goings.

Claire and Arthur were cordial, but Claire knew there wasn't anything warm and bonding between them. Too often his eyes looked narrow and evaluating. But those same eyes showed unabashed love toward Heather. Even so, that did not ease Claire's nagging doubts.

The wedding took place July 1st; Heather's 19th birthday. Arthur had insisted orchids from Hawaii be flown in and they were garlanded, common as weeds, throughout the winery and its reception hall. Claire remembered the conversation with Heather, sitting on their couch one day, regarding the choice of a winery over a church in which to be married.

"Arthur says it's European and he prefers that."

"We're American. Is that all he said about it?"

Quickly, Heather looked down and her hands nervously began smoothing the fabric of her purple and white flowered sundress. Her mouth worked awhile beneath scowling brows before she spoke. "He says common people marry in a church." Heather's voice wasn't much above a whisper as though she was ashamed to share this confession with Claire. "He says we're more than common. He says we're special, and we're going places in the world."

"Is that what you believe?"

Heather continued staring into her skirt folds, unconsciously tracing the pattern of one flower over and over. When she did raise her head to meet Claire's gaze, sadness covered her face. "No, Aunt Claire, I feel less special than most people. Maybe it goes back to never having a mom and dad and that old problem of feeling different as a child. That never made me feel special, it made me feel like a leftover, and like everybody was better than

I was. You and Arthur are the only people who have ever truly loved me."

"One day you will accept how special you are, Heather; and as for love, most of us in an entire lifetime can count true love from others on one hand. You can put your mom and dad on the list of those who loved you. Maybe the way to look at it is as how much love we give, instead of how much we receive."

Claire's thinking immediately pictured the glowing bouquet of red roses several years earlier and remembered the young Roy whom she believed loved Heather as sincerely as anyone could. "Have you and Arthur talked about God, and about a church being God's house?"

"He said Charles Darwin put the God issue to rest over a hundred years ago."

Claire wondered if Arthur contemplated the star-seeded Milky Way, or an orange butterfly sunbathing atop purple verbena.

"Some people don't want to submit to a loving but demanding God, Heather, because they prefer to follow their own will. That's why Charles Darwin's philosophy of evolution is so popular. It's a socially acceptable way to rebuke God's will." Claire decided one more question along these lines, and then Heather should be allowed her time of joy unhindered by concerns of existence and life eternal. "And you, Heather? Do you believe there is a God?"

Looking straight into Claire's eyes, she answered, "Yes," then shrugged her shoulders and they said no more.

You do not feed meat to an infant because they cannot chew and swallow solid food. First they work at fluids to take their nourishment, and only gradually learn the foods of life. You must be led by the unseen and drawn to the source before your purpose can begin.

Heather's wedding dress was white satin and lace with a sweetheart top, and a dazzling belt of crystal beads and silver sequins. Her extravagant train needed four flower girls to attend. A Justice of the Peace had been hired by Arthur to perform the ceremony. Claire wore a lilac-colored silk dress, with low-heeled shoes in silk to match. Because Heather wanted Claire "inside the ceremony" as she put it, Claire wore Heather's faceted garnet necklace, tied into flower shapes at intervals along its length. Claire caught herself fingering its smooth faceted surfaces frequently throughout the evening.

The event was well attended. Claire's acquaintances in the community were considerable, and Heather had a moderate circle of friends, but Arthur had none.

A hush fell over the crowd as the Wedding March began. Heather was glowing. Her ample red hair was swept atop her head and her bridal veil was adorned with real pearls at Arthur's insistence. It was like a stellar cloud around her red mane, with little planets of opaque white punctuating that red and white sky before streaming behind her like a jet stream brought softly to earth.

Heather's bouquet flowers were fresh from Hawaii and Oregon. Dozens of large white Trilliums were bunched in the middle of this large bouquet which was additionally punctuated with yellow and purple orchids. Light and airy, Asparagus plumosa ferns were artfully added to soften the overall effect.

Arthur, already standing before the Justice of the Peace, looked elegant in his white tuxedo, with white silk bow tie. One of his employees stood in for Best Man. Heather began her slow approach toward him as Arthur watched with pride. He seemed calm to Claire. The whispering of the crowd and comments about the beauty of the bride and gown escaped from people as Heather passed them on her way to unite her life with Arthur Conway. It was over quickly. Heather's voice was light and delicate, probably not audible much beyond the front row where Claire and Rose sat. Arthur on the other hand was heard to the last row and probably out into the street, in triumph it seemed to Claire.

The reception was similar to all receptions. Customs in a nation are customs in a nation, only larger and smaller in comparison to one another. This particular reception was large as a cosmic event.

Along with champagne from France, high-priced wines were offered by the glass, by the bottle, by the case, by the planet, by the galaxy, by stellar eternity, Claire thought. Hors d'oeuvres had been ordered through the famous David Myerhoffer & Company of New York and flown to the reception kitchen that morning in a refrigerated compartment of an airplane. A chef with an international reputation, who ruled a five-star restaurant in Europe, had been hired at great expense. Heather was too embarrassed to tell Claire how much the chef would be paid, so Claire hadn't pressed for an answer. The chef and his staff were instructed to prepare a banquet for 200 people.

In the reception hall, long tables were draped with purple linen and decorated with tall-stemmed crystal vases that presented the flower arrangements above the heads of those sitting across from one another. There were seven vases along every table. Each vase held a dozen flower-laden spikes of orchids in stunning yellow combinations, and from the center; lavender, purple, and magenta hydrangeas rose like an exquisite dawn.

The wine country grape theme echoed in the intricate details of Heather's decorating choices. Sparkling purple Swarovski crystals in the shape of a small grape cluster adorned the purple linen napkins at each table setting. These were gifts for the guests. The nine-tiered wedding cake was decorated with live purple grape clusters that ran as a meandering vine around the cake from top to bottom. At every turn the eyes met sumptuous grape adornments throughout the hall.

Pondering this extravagance, Claire hoped Arthur's video stores were prosperous.

Arthur's parents had arrived the evening before from Missouri, but seemed not to be present. They were shadowy in their movements and appeared uncomfortable. Both were plain people and from their appearance, not well-situated financially. There was shabbiness to their clothing that mirrored in their demeanor as embarrassment.

Mr. Conway shuffled as he walked and was permanently bent at the waist. Mrs. Conway was always just behind her husband, as though towed in his wake as a matter of physics more than choice. She kept her attention riveted on the ground most of the time and had given Claire only a furtive upward glance when they had been introduced prior to the wedding ceremony. Mr. Conway had simply offered Claire one rather violent thrust of a handshake and said 'Hello' with something like a grunt. After a few minutes of intense effort to converse with the Conway's, Claire gave up for sheer lack of response and drifted away from them because of their noticeable discomfort.

Claire didn't see Arthur speak to his parents, though several times in the evening she noticed Heather sitting with them, speaking with animation. Claire was too far across the room to know if they were responding well to their new daughter-in-law; but if they weren't, Heather was too excited and happy to notice.

The Conway's slipped away early, because not too much later Claire went looking for them in sympathy that they didn't know anyone and were probably feeling left-out and awkward. She didn't find them, so she went to Arthur and asked where his parents were. He turned to face her squarely. His face sobered from the gayness it had just been emanating to the crowd gathered around him. His back to that audience now, he addressed Claire privately in his high-pitched voice. "I sent them away."

At first Claire thought she had heard wrong. "I beg your pardon?"

"You heard right, Auntie, I sent them away."

This was the first salutation of "Auntie" Arthur had used in addressing her and she didn't like its hint of mockery, but for the moment the more important issue pertained to Arthur's parents. "May I ask why?"

"You may."

She waited.

Arthur moved his lips into their snarl shape. Claire had seen this expressions many times but was still uncertain if it was natural or conjured.

She waited, determined to hold her ground however long it took this young man to respond with whatever truth or lie he chose.

Finally, a harsh emotion passed over his face and in a vicious whisper he hissed, "They don't belong here!"

"Your parents don't belong at your wedding?"

He laughed low and sardonically.

Claire waited.

Arthur stepped closer to her. His adoring group of moments

before had melted into the milling crowd. "You saw them," he scoffed.

Her confusion was obviously because he chuckled, then added, "You are smitten by our wedding glamour, like my beautiful bride, Auntie, and haven't noticed certain facts."

Heather's new husband or not, she decided to be frank. "Arthur," she began, "First of all, I insist on being called Claire, not 'Auntie.' Furthermore, if you continue as though this were a quiz, I will flunk. Why don't you just say whatever it is you're trying to tell me?"

A glower passed over Arthur's face and a red flush, not of embarrassment Claire recognized, but of anger; the anger of coins spilling down the Temple steps, away from God.

He leaned his face inches from hers. She stood firmly, awaiting his reply.

"I sent them away because they're Hillbillies," he snapped, "is that plain enough?"

"Not yet," she answered calmly, hoping her shock wasn't apparent. "'Hillbilly' is a vague word. Can you be more specific?"

Arthur leaned his head back and gave a lusty laugh. Claire studied his upper palette and wondered if there was something there that made it greedier than most palettes that were already greedy enough.

He faced her again, lifting his thumb and forefinger to fidget with his moustache in downward strokes. Removing his hand, he continued, "My parents, and their parents, and their parents, and all the parents of all the generations of my parents forever, have been dirt farmers. Did you see my father's hands? They have been in the dirt so long they'll never come clean. And Mother? Did you see that mouse? She eats her cheese and bread at a worn out table every day of her life and looks worse than the table for wear. She takes what my father brings her from the fields and spends her life putting it into little jars, like a squirrel storing nuts. They do not laugh. They do not live. They are dirt poor Ozark farmers who don't know anything else. They're disgusting creatures and that is why I sent them away."

"Why did you bother to invite them in the first place?" Claire asked calmly, though stunned by what Arthur had just said.

"Your niece has a big compassionate heart. I'll even confide to you that my gorgeous bride and I had our first argument over inviting my parents. I said 'no' but my Turtle said 'yes'. She was close to giving me an ultimatum about having them here, so I relented rather than risk my bride-to-be's early wrath. Therefore they came and now they've gone, and you'll never have the misfortune of meeting them again." Arthur gave a mock salute, clacked his heels together and spun away from Claire to re-enter the crowd. Within moments he was vivaciously involved with the guests and slapping the backs of other men. Claire was aware that when he had turned, his coat tails had spun outward and slapped against her knees. The feeling had repulsed her as the ending sensation of the horrible confession he had just made.

Food tables along the walls were filled with exquisite offerings. Near the lengthy assortment of breads and rolls, cold cuts were offered: Italian prosciutto; thinly sliced salami; pheasant breast; roasted loin of veal; Black Forest ham. Huge varieties of hard cheese were followed by soft cheeses, some cut into pinwheels and stuffed with tomatoes, olives, and pureed garlic; hearts of palm; fennel and arugula; black truffle bordelaise; celery root and chestnut puree. Foie gras filled a porcelain container the actual shape and size of a live goose. There were boiled quail eggs placed between succulent stalks of white baby asparagus. Russian caviar was offered in large crystal bowls as was chilled oysters Rockefeller; and all the while French champagne and wine flowed at the rate of an overwrought river.

After these appetizers were enjoyed by the guests, the chef, a young man with cheeks puffed up from overeating, rolled a fully roasted pig, its mouth held ajar with the traditional apple, into the center of the room beneath the blazing chandelier. He clapped his hands for everyone's attention. "Ladies and gentlemen, please be seated."

After the commotion of settling into chairs, the chef held two enormous knives above his head. He began wielding them in what resembled an overhead duel. First he would run the blades along each other, separate them, then bring the metal together again with a clash, sweeping them along their lengths before separating them once more. After five or six repetitions of this maneuver he set his attention onto the roast pig before him.

He hesitated a moment, the long blades gleaming over his head, then brought the knives down in a tremendous rush and began the carving. Immediately, the aroma of pork roast succulence filled the room. The chef seemed a man crazed and even from Claire's table at a distance, she could see the glisten of perspiration gathering on his face as he worked. Occasionally, as though coming up for air, both knives would be raised overhead and stilled a moment before lunging downward again. A full twenty minutes passed in this magnificent frenzied performance, as the chef moved around the table agile as a gazelle, until at last the pig lay lean, its tender meat spread out in symmetrical designs fallen neatly away from the skeleton.

First wiping his knives then replacing those sabers into two leather scabbards, one on each side of his belt, the chef bowed toward Heather and Arthur, whose table had been moved to be near this display. Noticeably, Heather blushed and beamed. Certainly, no one failed to enjoy this live artful performance, and heartfelt applause was offered.

The employed staff began rolling out additional trays of steaming foods. The women wore black dresses that reached just above the knees, and white Battenberg lace aprons. A bow of the same lace was attached at the back of their heads, its panels streaming to shoulder length as a feminine touch of beauty. They lined up their offerings after a table that held warmed gold-rimmed white China plates and shiny golden silverware, then stood with ready smiles to assist. The chef rolled the pork to where it would be the first main-course offering. Next came prime rib; stuffed chicken breasts; lamb; dumplings the size of peaches; deep fried potatoes pieces in coiled shape, and mashed garlic cream-cheese potatoes. Gravies of pork, beef, and chicken followed, then grilled cod fish; salmon; trout; butter poached lobster; steaming clams; and escargot. There were cold and hot potato salads; sauerkrauts of various colors; jellied aspic; pickled pearl onions and mandarin oranges nestled in small exotic lettuces topped with citrus vinaigrette; tomatoes stuffed with shrimp cream filling; and many food trays beyond these.

Claire took a small sample of everything along the way until her plate was too full to add more. Looking at the sumptuous feast on her dish as she returned to her table, she wondered if one stomach could hold even this much, though her imaginary appetite would have been delighted to return for a sample of the remaining savory foods.

There was a general air of goodwill as the crowd sat down to this plentiful food offering. Rose had attended the wedding alone since her husband was out of town on business and as these best friends sat together they began comparing the contents on each other's plates. "Our tastes are similar," Claire noted.

"I've always known that, but where did they get these quail eggs?" Rose wondered aloud before pulling one from her fork into her heart-shaped mouth. After relishing the quail egg, she continued, "By the way, I introduced myself to Arthur's parents, then noticed they left early. Was there a problem?"

"Arthur made a confession to me this evening."

Rose stopped eating and leaned forward with her elbows atop the table. She placed her right index finger above her top lip and her thumb against her jaw, then looked kindly into Claire's eyes. Claire knew this was her professional and possibly unconscious gesture of studying and evaluating a person as she readied herself for professional exchange. Whenever Claire saw Rose take this stance she knew the wheels of an intelligent mind were at work to perceive and make a judgment call.

"He called his parents 'dirt farmers' and if not for Heather he wouldn't have invited them. He sent them away as soon as he could, then told me he hoped I would never have to see them again." Claire stopped and helped herself to a mouthful of creamed shrimp before asking Rose, "What does it mean?"

"It's easy," Rose answered, "Money is his god."

"What does that mean for Heather?'

"Trouble."

Claire lowered her fork. "What kind of trouble?"

Rose took in the room with a sweeping gesture of her eyes. "This is only the beginning, Claire. Heather's new husband is extravagant. We've been to countless weddings and don't you agree this is the most lavish display we've ever seen?"

"Without question."

"That's what I mean by 'trouble'." Rose tapped her crystal goblet bubbling with champagne. "Heather won't be able to control Arthur's expensive tastes."

Claire gazed over Rose's shoulder and saw Heather and Arthur at the center table with their heads close together and smiling into one another's face as though they were the only people on earth. Claire found it hard to imagine their happiness could ever turn sad. "The joyful moments are brief, aren't they Rose?" she said in a dream-like way, not taking her eyes off Heather who now tilted her beautiful head back and laughed at something Arthur had said.

"Very. However, the problem is fueled by believing life should be continuously joyful. Defining happiness realistically within our given human state is the beginning of healthy thinking."

"Come on, give," Claire teased.

Rose smiled. "Free advice?"

"Yes. Give."

"Find your ability; pursue it; persist; and never give up. Don't expect to double over with laughter too many times in a life. Be honest. Accept weaknesses in people as well as in yourself." Rose smiled sweetly, "Appreciate creation and try desperately to love others."

"That's it?"

"That's one side."

"And the other?"

"The other side is more complex because it's about a plethora of values. They're more difficult to change once they're ingrained."

"Like money values?"

"Yes, that, and countless other ways of looking at life and the world. Sometimes values pair up and take on greater strength. It's the principle of synergism."

"Is that Arthur's problem?" Claire inquired.

Rose tapped the gold rimmed goblet again. "Probably. The video stores must be a gold mine or Arthur will have trouble paying for this wedding feast. It's a downward spiral that sucks harder and harder until it's out of control. I've seen many people in my office broken because of money." Rose sighed deeply. "There aren't many Gandhi's, or Sister Teresa's walking upon the earth, Claire. Instead we have lots of greedy people and lots of materialistic people and an amazing number of unhappy people who believe their well-being is to be found in tangible things. We're all guilty of it in varying degrees. But those rare souls like Gandhi and Sister Teresa are pinnacles of the highest values minus materialism. Did you know Sister Teresa gave up everything material to devote her life to the sick and starving orphans of Calcutta? Earlier, while a Sister in a convent there, she was granted permission to take a wheelbarrow into the Calcutta streets and remove the dead bodies because society didn't allow people to touch them. Corpses were left where they took their last breath, typically in the streets. That was her beginning in India, long before she established her orphanage and hospital for children."

"The differences in people are shocking, aren't they, Rose."

"As a psychiatrist I see unending types and I'm tempted to say 'yes,' but there's an underlying sameness to all problems, which leads me to say 'no'. It's all a matter of right and wrong values and the choices associated with them."

"Heather has never been concerned about money," Claire offered. "I know she and Arthur had some sharp discussions regarding the wedding because she wanted to use her family savings for a down payment on a house. When her parents died, Heather became the sole heir of slightly more than $200,000.00, which has been invested carefully and conservatively on her behalf until she reached 21, or until she married if she was 19 years of age or older. Well, today is her 19th birthday, Rose, so besides this being her marriage day, it is also the day of her inheritance. Arthur spent almost $50,000.00 of it on what you see here. The paperwork to turn over her assets will only take a few days, so meanwhile everything was charged to be paid soon by what used to be conservative investments and that now have become gold-rimmed goblets; these gorgeous orchids flown in from Hawaii; a roast pig with an apple in its mouth; foie gras; and all the riches of this Cinderella night. Heather's wedding dress cost over $10,000.00.

"He told Heather they'll only get married once so it should be a wedding of splendor.

"I fought Heather to keep her wedding simple and her inheritance intact, and even though she stood up to Arthur, he won the argument. If I could legally put a stop to spending her inheritance like this, I would!" Anger welled up inside Claire about this puppeteer, Arthur, who had cleverly set their wedding to the timing of Heather's inheritance. She quaked inside and felt almost vicious, like she was a hot branding iron and wanted to strike Arthur in the face. It surprised her to realize she was capable of such dark thoughts.

Rose shook her head in a 'no' motion, then looked up at Claire and smiled her heart shaped lips in their pleasant winning way. "Up to a point, life's lessons and hardships are good for character development, but if the doses become too high they can cause destruction. Let's hope Heather's future will be on this side of that limit."

Again Claire noticed the jubilant young couple, now beginning the first dance of the evening under the dimmed chandelier. Their noses were touching and Arthur's lips moved with words for Heather alone. In those moments they knew nothing of crystal goblets and values, of inheritances or a roast pig. They were fresh-blooded hearts, eager to join.

Chapter Nine

Dear Aunt Claire,

*I can't believe I'm Mrs. Arthur Conway! Here we are on the
40th floor of the White Swan in Las Vegas. The room is on a
corner of the building with windows from the ceiling to the floor
so you look out from two sides. It's like living in the sky. I didn't
know there were so many lights in the whole world. The electric
billboards blink and become pictures and shapes and change
colors. It's exciting. The energy bills here must be shocking. I
feel like a little girl in a fairy tale, and I have my prince. Aunt
Claire, he is the most wonderful husband. He loves me more
than I can say. I didn't know I could feel this way. We will be
happy forever and ever. That's what he tells me and I believe
him! I'll only love him more each day. We shopped yesterday
and Arthur bought me a bright orange jumpsuit, "To compliment
my hair", he said. It's an original, one of a kind, and it was very
expensive. To tell you the truth Aunt Claire...and I would never
say this to Arthur because it might hurt his feelings...I don't like
it. It's so bright that people stare at me. It pleases Arthur, so I
act like I love it too, and maybe I will learn to like it. It's just that
when people stare that much at me I feel uncomfortable,
especially when it's the men. I wore it to dinner tonight and
never had so much attention in my life. It's surprising how easy
it is to get people to look at you. Oh well, Arthur's happy and
that's what counts.*

*We ate at the top of a hotel with a restaurant that rotates one full
circle every hour so you get a complete view of Las Vegas. We
both had lobster tail with drawn butter. The lobsters were flown
in alive all the way from Maine this morning. Mine was a little
tough so I think it was stressed from the travel. I didn't say
anything and Arthur seemed to love his. Maybe his lobster was a
better traveler than mine!*

We went to a show after dinner. I wore my new jumpsuit, and Arthur was in a black silk shirt and black western slacks. He even wore his new cowboy boots. He looked so cute. Anyway, I was shocked! Arthur said he's seen things like that show before and everybody that comes to Las Vegas goes to topless shows, but that didn't make me feel any better. It was embarrassing with all those half-dressed women and their tall feather hats strutting back and forth. After all, my husband is a man and why do those women need to be half-naked? They didn't do anything but walk around with fixed smiles. I only know I didn't care for it, but Arthur seemed to enjoy himself and kissed my fingers a lot, so I guess it's all right. I hope he won't want to go to another one of those shows again while we're here this week.

Love,
Heather

Dear Aunt Claire,

Arthur loves the black jack game and I don't know a thing about it, so last night after standing behind his chair watching him for hours, until my feet burned, I came upstairs and soaked in the tub, then wrote to you and went to bed. He came in hours later. I asked how he did and he mumbled something about a bad streak then fell like a timber onto the bed. It's almost noon and he is fast asleep. He's snoring. Even his snoring is cute! Tonight we're going to another show. Some actress is singing and he said I'd like her because she has red hair. I don't know what that's supposed to mean. He also insists I wear that orange jumpsuit again. It's so noticeable, that anyone who saw it last night and sees me again will think I don't have anything else to wear. I'm beginning to really dislike that outfit, but Arthur's happiness is more important, so I'll wear it and try not to notice the men looking at me. I wonder why their staring doesn't bother Arthur?

Love,
Heather

Dear Aunt Claire,

Arthur is downstairs playing black jack again. Tonight was awful. The red-haired actress played the piano and sang. She had a tube of oxygen attached to the microphone so vapor was always rising from her mouth. It looked like she was steaming. I never heard of a singer needing oxygen to sing. She banged the piano keys, and yelled more than sang, and I was bored by her constantly asking the light man for a special light from his control room so she could put her hand into the beam and make her huge diamond ring splash rainbows over the walls of the room. Once of that was enough. Besides her terrible performance, the orange jumpsuit was more uncomfortable than ever. It scratches at the neck where the label is real big with that designer's name. But Arthur was happy and that's what counts.

After the singer with the oxygen tube, unfortunately, we went back to that show where the women on stage don't wear much. An actor, a man in a safari outfit, came out and grabbed one of those women and tied her to a phony stake they had wheeled to the middle of the stage. I guess it was supposed to mean he was going to burn her at the stake or something. Anyway, she struggled to get loose and screamed her lungs out just like it was real. Then he pulled out a whip and pretended to whip her. It was stupid, but Arthur laughed. He thought it was funny. "Great show, great show," he kept saying. I wish he had noticed I wasn't saying much about it and asked how I felt, but he was having such a good time he didn't see how unhappy I was. Here he comes...I hear his key in the door. I hope his luck was good. We'll be home in two days. See you soon.

Love,
Heather

It was a somber redhead that stopped by two days later. She was alone. "Hi, Aunt Claire."

"Welcome home, newlywed. How was your honeymoon?"

"Parts of it were okay." Heather lifted her palms into the air with a gesture of helplessness. "Other parts I could have lived without."

They settled into the breakfast nook with its rectangular maple

100

table. For minutes Heather sat quietly, drumming her fingers against the surface and staring placidly into the back yard with its close-cropped grassy expanse, then a long row of St. Joseph's roses in their many-colored bloom, and behind that several flowering orange trumpet vines scrambling over the rear fence. Twittering birds could be heard through the screens where the windows had been pushed up to allow the passage of fresh air into the room. An ancient Mimosa Silk tree stood in the center of the lawn. Pink tropical-bird-like flowers stood up from the top of its wide canopy as branching dappled the yard with shade through its delicate ferny leaves. This tree had always been Heather's favorite because of its fuzzy pink pastel blooms, but also because it closed its leaves at night until each cluster resembled a lean string bean. Then the following morning it would unfurl again into lacy strands. Not often was the active life in a plant so robust and noticeable.

Claire fixed coffee but didn't speak, knowing Heather had something important on her mind and would share when the time was right. For the moment staring into what had been her happy childhood world was a dose of what Claire guessed was good medicine for her.

She placed her steaming mug on the table and sat down, looking in the same direction out the window as Heather, then took the first sip of her coffee.

"I don't know what to do, Aunt Claire." It was a flat, quiet, but tumultuous statement and Claire knew it came from a deep place, where a little movement disturbs an entire place of its peace and quiet. It was as though a block of internal earth was adjusting its foundational body and caused a scraping howl in the bowels of the earth where it originated, but which was not heard at first on the surface. As that struggle worked its way upward, it eventually shuddered the ground above and continued upward through basements and living rooms and attics until it reached the end of the material world and kept going along with the added sounds of breakage and screams until it died away into the sky, having forever forged a new page of history.

Claire knew the moment she heard the tone of Heather's voice some shift of epic magnitude had occurred. She waited, knowing it had to be Heather's decision when to say what she needed to share.

Heather took both her hands and ran them back from her forehead, gathering her long curly red locks and twisting the bundle in that mysterious way Claire had never understood, so that all Heather's hair stayed in a shiny red knot at the back of her head. She looked at Claire, with her amber eyes noticeably dulled, and bluntly stated, "Arthur is in trouble."

"What kind of trouble?"

"Money trouble."

"So soon?" Claire thought, but answered instead, "What type of money trouble?"

"Serious trouble."

"Can you be more specific?"

Heather swung her attention out toward the yard again. Claire had never seen Heather's profile more somber. "He lost a lot of money at blackjack."

Carefully, Claire asked, "How much is 'a lot'?"

How deep is your basement? How strong is your dungeon? What time is it? Careful, or the quicksand will grab your ankles.

Heather bit her lower lip and Claire noticed how red the left corner of Heather's lip appeared and realized it had been the victim of Heather's anxiety. "$40,000.00," she answered flatly, then swung her wide-eyed attention onto Claire. "We have already spent so much of my inheritance for the wedding, and now, when the money comes I have to pay Arthur's gambling debt besides all the things we charged for our wedding. Then my inheritance will be less than half, but..." she stopped suddenly.

"But what?" Claire gently urged.

"Aunt Claire! This isn't what my mother and father would have wanted. Their hard-earned money was never meant to pay a gambling debt! I wanted to make a down payment on a house for Arthur and me. What am I going to do?" Heather broke into convulsive sobs. Her hair loosened from its captivity and fell around her lowered face like a tent of red shame.

For a moment, Claire was silent, debating whether or not she should share her thoughts under these extreme circumstances of desperation. She decided to voice her thinking. "Perhaps you should re-arrange your bank records so you alone have control over your inheritance money."

Heather looked up and stared before speaking. "Aunt Claire!

I couldn't! I love Arthur too much! Besides, Arthur says everything that's his is mine and everything that's mine is his. I have to help him."

"How can you be sure he won't do it again?"

"He promised!" Heather responded enthusiastically. "He held me and cried like a baby. He felt so bad, and solemnly swore that after this debt is paid he will never let it happen again."

"And you believe him?"

"I know he's telling the truth. He said the thrill of getting married and all the casino excitement made him feel crazy. I wish you could have seen him, Aunt Claire. He was so sorry. I know it was an accident. I've been worried to tell you because I want you to love Arthur. He loves me, and that's what counts, isn't it?" It was a pleading more than a question.

"Yes, of course."

"I'll have $90,000.00 left after the honeymoon and the gambling debt and the cost of our wedding and my ring. That's still enough to make a down payment on a little house. Tonight I'm going to talk to Arthur about that."

They continued visiting through the afternoon. It was obvious to Claire that Heather was at first making a conscious effort to be her former self, but as the hours passed she became more relaxed and natural. Before leaving, Heather gathered a few more items from her bedroom. Her move into Arthur's apartment had taken minimal effort since it was already lavishly furnished with Arthur's belongings.

The following morning the phone rang and Claire excused herself from the client she was helping to find affordable living, and was happy to hear Heather's cheerful voice on the other end of the connection.

"Aunt Claire, I wanted you to know that last night Arthur and I had a long serious talk and decided whatever we have, money or anything, belongs equally to both of us. He likes the idea of getting a house, but what is left of my inheritance won't buy a very big house and Arthur is not for that. We decided to leave the money in the bank and try to add to it until we have enough for a nice home. We're both happy with that decision and I hope you are happy too."

A heavy feeling started in Claire, a feeling that she was

103

sinking into deep murky waters where her opinions and ideas and concerns came forth only as bubbles that wiggled to the surface and popped without making a sound. She knew what she had to say. "I'm glad you and Arthur worked it out, Heather; I only hope Arthur has the strength and honor to leave the money untouched."

"Oh, he does, Aunt Claire. I know he does."

Claire didn't answer because she didn't believe Arthur could restrain himself.

Chapter Ten

The years passed, and Heather grew more beautiful. Maturing fit well on her. The bubbling of youth had settled into a quiet calm energy. She was 22 and had worked three years with Arthur at their video stores. Heather and Arthur stopped by Claire's every Sunday afternoon, usually around 2 p.m., after Claire returned from church services and visiting someone in the hospital or perhaps a lonely soul without family or a friend in the world that cared. Claire felt humbled and blessed after these outings.

Occasionally, sitting at a stop light, she noted the cars lined up behind and in front of her with animated conversations common as a house spider between busy mothers at the wheel and a child or two or three with her in the vehicle; or the music blaring too loud from a driver's window; or teen-age girls laughing hysterically over what Claire suspected was some minor provocation; she saw married couples, young and old; the obvious work vehicles; and office workers with starched collars. All this was the movement and commotion of life's endless flow, while her particular mission took her to a place that was a detour; a dead end some might call it. Her purpose was to reach this barely inhabited ramble. Here, there was no rush and roar of human activity. Here, there was pain and fear and loneliness. Even if the hurrying crowd was invited, they would continue to pass by on their own courses, driven and selfish.

Claire wondered why more people didn't care about the elderly who were so often discarded like old shoes. "Their significance is over, Claire! It's a bright New World! There are important errands! Hurry! The sale is 20% off! Don't be late! The football game, the soccer match, the tee-off is at 8 a.m. Fast now! The Big Top is in town. The high wire is about to begin; without a net! Quick! The thrills, the wanton empty thrills; the calories that don't nourish; the sticky sugars that jitter the body without feeding it. Rush! We won't miss life, by golly! We'll live it up. Isn't there a saying that today we feast for tomorrow we die? Grab it while there's time. Grab it all. Stuff your pockets and your cheek pouches. Fill your closets and all the empty spaces you can find. Get happiness! Get! Get! Get!"

Claire walked into the Golden Age Rest Home, then through a large room with furniture arranged for conversing and watching the fireplace. There were magazines on the end tables, and the morning newspaper lay in neatly folded sections after having been read, then placed next to a cage on the main large center table within which perched two yellow canaries huskily singing like proclamations of the Second Coming.

She continued down the hallway toward room 107. There were several elderly ladies sitting on a wall-couch who stopped talking as she neared and returned her greeting as she passed. She knew her presence was variety in a day that otherwise was like every other day, without breaks or distinctions to mark one as unique from another. It was Thanksgiving and Claire knew one thoroughly sweet and ill widow without family. She had taken great care to pick the most beautiful cut flowers at the florist and have them arranged in the shape of a peacock's tail in order that it could be placed against the wall rather than work as a centerpiece needing four good visual sides. Yellow gladiolas; cherry colored Peruvian lilies; copper bearded iris, red gerbera daisies, white baby's breath, and some delicate purple sage blossoms made up the body of the arrangement. As a last flare, the florist, a quiet gray-haired woman with thick glasses and bony hands, had deftly stuck some Maple twigs cloaked in their rusty autumn colors into tiny green tubes that looked like needle syringes, where water lay waiting to help sustain the plant's severance from the parent body.

The colors worked nicely as a tribute to autumn and Thanksgiving, Claire thought as she carried the floral offering into the room. A woman's round face, yellowed by illness, and surrounded by short salt-and-pepper colored hair looked up from her book and beamed when she saw Claire and the bouquet.

"Happy Thanksgiving, Betty."

"You are a saint."

"There's not a person I know who loves flowers more than you."

Betty smiled with the most sparkling smile Claire ever saw on a human face.

Eagerly, Betty listened as Claire described each flower according to what she knew and what the florist had taught her. The flowers were placed against the wall across from the foot of the bed where Betty could see them easily, then the two ladies settled down to a quiet visit. Typically stoic about her health, today Betty was talkative regarding her illness. "You know, Claire, I'm supposed to be dead. Over a year ago, my doctors said the cancer was beyond anything they could treat, especially since it was in the liver. They told me I would die within six months. But I'm still here and do you know what's best of all?"

"What's that?"

"I'm not mad at God anymore."

"I didn't know you had been mad at him."

"Oh, I was! Fist shaking mad! But we had it out I guess you could say, until I accepted the fact that everyone has to die. If it isn't cancer it's something else. The time comes for everyone. 'It is appointed unto man once to die and then the judgment' is what the Bible teaches us."

"Then you're at peace?"

Betty was quiet a moment as her attention wandered back to the bouquet. Claire saw her eyes tracing the various flowers. "Yes I am, except..."

Claire waited.

Betty shifted her attention to the nearby window. A rectangle glass about three feet wide and reaching from ceiling to floor offered an outside view where a bed of purple and orange pansies lay colorfully under the autumn sun. From there, a sweep of short-mown lawn encircled a silver blue Mock pine tree before ending at the street, along which a few automobiles slowly traveled. Betty focused on Claire again.

"...except the nights are hard. When you've been with one man like I was with Frank for 65 years and knew he was beside me in the night, it's hard not to find him there anymore. I still reach for him, then wake up and realize where I am. That's the worst part. I never get used to not having him with me." She looked Claire in the face, an obvious glisten over her eyes. "I never stop missing him, and that's what makes me feel so alone in my illness. The being alone, Claire, is so awful. I wouldn't feel this way if Frank was here." Betty wiped the tears that sprang from her eyes. "Forgive me. You've been so kind to bring me flowers and I'm blubbering about my troubles."

"You're not blubbering. If we can't talk to one another about what's in our hearts we may as well be rocks."

If the bud doesn't open, it dies without the intended herald. If we walk through life and ignore the call to be all we are meant to be, the aftermath is a wasteland.

"The good Lord knew what he was doing to take Frank first," Betty continued, a more cheerful note in her voice. "Even though it's hard, I can take being alone better than he would have. There's blessing in that." Betty took a deep breath, "And I'm overdue, so Frank doesn't have long to wait." Betty smiled her beautiful smile and chuckled, "but I plan to keep on outliving the doctor's predictions, so no harp strings yet."

Claire knew that Betty was a feisty personality. This quiet gentle woman had a fighting spirit. It was harmless as a puppy, but it knew how to growl.

"It's intriguing, isn't it?" Claire ventured, "How sometimes we wonder if living is worth the effort, yet we always want to live, and we fight to live. I think we love life more than we realize. What do you think?"

"Yes, even when that means being alone." She swept her hand to encompass the room and somehow include the whole building and the entire world. "The staff is wonderful and the other old-timers like me are friendly. The food is good in the dining room. Have you seen that place?"

"Fancy."

Betty chuckled. "It's like a little five-star restaurant. Some of the men wear suits to dinner. The tablecloths are real linen, and we ladies get to dress up and wear our pearls; though outside our restaurant, you don't see so many canes, and walkers, and oxygen tanks alongside tables." Betty shifted in her bed then grimaced.

Claire was on her feet at once. "May I do something?"

Betty leaned her head back, closing her eyes a moment. "Hand me that control panel on the table, please."

Claire handed Betty the control. She took it into her hands

without moving her head or opening her eyes. It was obvious she knew the device by memory and didn't hesitate to push a button that lowered her bed from a sitting to a more prone position. Claire moved her chair closer to lessen the effort Betty needed to see her.

"The kidneys aren't doing so well. When I sit up too long they give such pain it blots out everything until I lie down."

She looked into Claire's face with tired, sad eyes. The upper lids wrinkled into folds atop her eyes, and the sallow facial skin matched the yellow tone of her neck and arms. Claire knew this was coloring from her cancerous liver. Betty's voice was weaker and more gravelly when she spoke again. "Frank was an angel. If the slightest muscle hurt on me he would nearly rub me away trying to make it feel better. Once, after he worked my aching leg for nearly an hour, I made him stop so he wouldn't end up sore himself. He wanted 'to make me last' is how he put it. He always told me he needed me to live because he couldn't live without me.

"You know, Claire, when I first lost Frank, it was hard not to hate myself for every harsh word I ever said to him in our years together. It was surprising how my memory picked up those minor times and clung to them."

"Thank the Lord for Father Brown. He comes Sundays to visit his 'flock' as he calls us, and learned from one of the ladies here that I was depressed and not eating much. He stopped in and before I knew it, I told him everything. He fixed me right there and then. He said Jesus Christ already paid the price for the times I wasn't kind to Frank. All I had to do was ask Jesus to take my sins and forgive me, and he would. I can't describe how that helped me. Father Brown gave me Holy Communion that day and ever since, even though I miss Frank as much as ever, it's only the good times I remember now.

"Faith is that way."

"Every week, Father Brown pops in to see me. So many residents here don't have visitors, and he's like a bunch of people coming all at once with his cheerful personality. I don't know why people talk so badly about preachers and churches. People from the churches do a lot to help people like me. I'm sorry to say it, but a lot of times preachers and men and women from the churches do more for old people than even their own relatives."

"I think people and families and even societies need their scapegoat," Claire answered. "The church has always been a favorite target for non-believers. The ones that mock don't understand what goes on under the church roof, and how much reaching out to help others goes forth every day by countless people who believe Christ's command to never tire of being kind."

"I don't suppose they'll ever know."

"Some will, some won't, but what counts is that kindness continues in spite of the world's criticism and hatred."

Betty winced again, quickly moving her hand to press against her right side.

"Can I do anything to help?"

"I better take a little nap."

Hastily, Claire stood. She leaned over and gave Betty a kiss on the forehead. "When the pain passes, remember all the Thanksgivings you and Frank shared that were wonderful. That will keep you busy until I come back next week."

Betty smiled, but didn't open her eyes. "Thank you for the flowers," she ended.

Exiting the room, Claire shut the door quietly behind her. Up and down the hallway were white-haired ladies making their way slowly with the help of walkers. Sometimes these elders were silent as Claire passed because the effort of moving along took their total concentration. Nonetheless, Claire always smiled and offered a "Hello", knowing it was a good seed to throw.

She pushed through the front doors into the cool bronze day. An elderly man sat on a bench outside, smoking a cigarette. Next to him, detached for now, was his portable oxygen supply. "Happy Thanksgiving," she offered.

"Those women drive me crazy," he answered, gesturing toward the Golden Age Rest Home's front doors.

"Well, that's not a bad way to go crazy," Claire answered cheerfully.

"I'm not so sure," he grumbled in what Claire knew was an artificial show of being gruff. She laughed and continued toward her station wagon.

The Misstep of Heather Bainbridge

It was 2 p.m. when Claire pulled into the driveway at home. Heather and Arthur hadn't yet arrived for their Sunday visit.

Claire stood several moments at the sidewalk and looked the length of her street. It blazed with autumn leaves of cinnamon red. A gust of wind passed and Claire watched leaves break loose then tumble and loop in their perennial dance, to settle at the feet of their parent. There they would lay and gradually break down into nutritious components to feed the life within the bark. Then upon the boughs, once again in spring, leaves would emerge as new aspiring surfaces in keeping with their mysterious code of shape and size and purpose, and hang upon the branch for another season under the sun. Claire knew this cycle would go on and on until long after the memory of her was vanished from the earth.

Approaching the front door, she saw an envelope taped to it and drawing closer recognized Heather's stationary; a light green envelope within which Claire knew would be light green paper with small yellow Roses twining across the top. Entering the house, Claire appreciated the warmth of the interior. She put her things down, then sat at the maple kitchen table and opened Heather's letter. After reading the first sentence, she laid it down. Looking quietly at the ceiling, she took a deep breath, then lifted the letter and began to read again.

Chapter Eleven

Dear Aunt Claire,

I have no one to turn to but you. I know you must have noticed that lately our visits on Sundays have been shorter? Arthur doesn't want to come at all but it's one of the few times I insist against his wishes. I know that I am right. Please don't think poorly of him, Aunt Claire. He never wants to see anyone, unless it's his friends at the race track on Sunday. It isn't you, it's anyone. He says he never gets to do anything because of our video business taking so much time so when he does have a day off he wants to be with his friends. I guess he's right, so we agreed to compromise. Some time with you, then I go home and do housework, and he goes to see his friends. Is it fair? I guess it is.

But that's not why I'm writing today. We have a problem. Please tell me if this is too much of a burden for you. You're the only one I have, besides Arthur, to talk to. Otherwise, I think I would go crazy because I feel as though there are nothing but problems, one after another. Forgive me if I never have happy things to talk about. It doesn't end; the hectic work and always getting things for the house. By the way, Arthur was so excited about your $20,000.00 loan to help us furnish our new home. It's so big compared to our first house. Since my inheritance is spent, the car, that fancy Jaguar sedan Arthur bought for so much money, can no longer be fixed because the repairs are too expensive. It's in the garage covered with a tarp because he couldn't sell it for half the money he paid for it. That darn machine took the last nickel of my parents' money. In a way, it was the final straw to make me a pauper. Aunt Claire, I'm wandering and I want to get to the point.

Arthur is gone, and only a few moments ago I found a note in his jeans pocket. It was addressed to Arthur and signed by someone name 'Georgie Boy.' The writer didn't come right out and say what he wanted to say. Everything was said 'between the lines' as the expression goes, but it was threatening. I'm scared, Aunt Claire. I think Arthur is in trouble. Here's what the paper said: 'Arthur, kid, you got no time left cuz Georgie Boy don't like lame ponies. They run or they die. Got it?'

For three or four months Arthur has been acting different. He's always nervous. I talk the way I always do but sometimes he jumps as though he heard a sudden loud noise behind him. He's also started yelling in his sleep. At first I would wake him, but then I decided to let him go through it, hoping it would tell me something about his predicament. Usually the word 'ponies' comes out from his nightmares, which I know is his track slang for the race-horses. He was screaming 'dead meat' last week then shielded his head and yelled, 'Get away! Get away!' His screaming woke him up. He was covered in perspiration and breathing hard. I asked him what the dream was about but he mumbled, 'Just a dream,' then turned over and went back to sleep.

I've learned over these years with Arthur that he has something like personality compartments. His race-track life, for example, is one part, and he doesn't share that with me. I always ask when he comes home on Sunday evenings how the races went. He answers, "Fine," and that's the end of it. I know men don't verbalize as well as women, but Arthur could say more than just one word. Then there are his work parts, which we do share since we're either in the same store or on the phone talking business between stores. And of course, our private lives are most special, at least for me, and the most wonderful part of my marriage to Arthur. He gives all his love to me. When Arthur comes to stand right in front of me, inches away, and brushes my hair back with his hands, then cups my face on both sides and tilts it upward to meet his kisses...you can't know how that makes me feel. I love him so much. He makes me feel like a princess. I wonder if two people have ever told one another how much they love each other as much as Arthur and I do. I'm sure Anthony and Cleopatra couldn't have been more deeply in love, even if they did go together on a big boat with sterling silver oars and perfume in the sails. They took actors and musicians along for entertainment, but if that had been Arthur and me, we would have made sure to go alone because each other is enough. But I'm straying again.

I'm worried about that note. It's frightening, and I don't know what to do. All his yelling in his sleep hasn't revealed anything to me except that he's disturbed, and I know it's not my imagination when I say he has dark circles under his eyes. Arthur is not the same person. Will you please call me when you finish reading this?

Love,
Heather

The phone rang almost the instant Claire finished the letter. It was Heather. "I couldn't wait any longer, Aunt Claire. What do you think?"

"Hello, Heather. First of all, a technical question. Why didn't Arthur let you stay today for our visit while he went his way since you were here to leave the note anyway?"

"I took the bus to your place then rode it home again. Arthur was like a blind man this morning. He didn't see how upset I was about not coming to see you. He said he had some important business to do at work right away, and to call and tell you I'll be there some other Sunday. Then he left.

"I knew you were at church then visiting Betty at the Rest Home, but I couldn't stand waiting, so I wrote the letter then rode the bus across town. The movement of doing something helped. How does it sound, Aunt Claire? Do you think Arthur is in trouble?"

"It's possible. Who do you think this Georgie Boy is?"

"I'm sure it's the man Arthur talks to in the other room. Whenever a certain man calls and I answer all I hear is chewing, like he has a piece of gum in his mouth, and finally he'll say 'gimme Arthur' in a rough voice. Arthur takes those calls in his office where I can't hear him and he waits very carefully to make sure I've hung up before he starts talking to the man. I can never hear the words, but sometimes Arthur gets loud and angry talking to him. Lately, I've heard him slam the phone down after the man calls, then sit quiet as a stone in his office for hours."

"Heather, the man calling could be a bookie or someone from the mob world."

"A what?"

"A bookie, someone who takes bets for gambling. I think that's how it works."

"Why wouldn't Arthur place his own bets?"

"Either he pays the bookie because he believes the bookie has some inside information that will pay off, or..." Claire hesitated, knowing she had to warn her niece about what she feared was true.

"Or what, Aunt Claire?"

"Or maybe they go into debt with the bookie or someone else maybe. I suppose you could call it a loan. He may owe money that he can't pay back."

Heather was quiet on the other end of the telephone for several moments. "What does he mean about lame ponies and they run or they die," she asked carefully.

"It sounds like a threat."

"Because Arthur owes him money?"

"Maybe."

"You mean Arthur's life may be in danger? Aunt Claire! Please come over!"

"I'll leave now, Heather."

Hanging up, Claire remembered the lonely serenity of the Golden Age Rest Home compared to this churning human dilemma and felt astonished by how vast the differences in human paths and plights could be. The red and bronze pansies lining the borders of the shale walkway seemed to bow their faces in sorrow as Claire hurried by.

Fifteen minutes later she pulled up to a rambling ranch style home that sat on a knoll overlooking Walnut Glen. Fuchsia pink when in season, miniature ice-plants carpeted the slope until the view lifted again into the distant low rolling hills covered in horizontal lines that Claire knew represented viticulture in this warm, richly-soiled California valley.

Heather and Arthur's mailbox glinted solid brass under the sun. Heather was on the front porch and hurried to Claire's car door. She was sobbing.

"Now, now, Heather, we don't know for sure. This could be a simple misunderstanding."

"Arthur just called. I can't believe it! He said he's not coming home tonight because he loves me! Aunt Claire, what's going on?"

"Let's go inside. We'll figure this out." She led her sobbing red haired child-by-proxy into the spacious house. As always when Claire entered this home, the expensive furnishings amazed her. They crossed the Picasso marble entryway, then passed the dining room to the left with its 7-tiered crystal chandelier hanging over a cherry-wood table with eight tufted needle-point chairs to match, each with an elaborate fox-chase scene. A silk runner lay along the table's center and orchids of tiny yellow flowers with red throats stood in the middle with four foot spikes laden with blooms. Claire knew Arthur insisted on fresh orchids in bloom all year. After their flowering cycle Claire was given the plants which she tended until a new blooming came, after which she would give the plant to someone, usually in a nursing home or at the hospital. The plants had easily numbered in the hundreds because Arthur liked them situated throughout the range of his and Heathers' plush expansive dwelling.

They approached the room with a south facing wall glassed from floor to ceiling and tinted in a golden hue. Here, the scenery was like a fan, spread and hand-painted. The slope trailing from the house down to a glittering creek was covered thickly in miniature blue periwinkle intermixed with ground hugging yellow daisies. Indigenous Manzanita and Toyon trees populated the opposite side of the brook, as Steller's blue jays fluttered between their branches squawking loudly as though in protest over some indignant law aimed at Steller's jays.

The living room carpet was white and deep and clean. Shoes were left at the beginning of this room where an assortment of slippers was offered. Claire and Heather switched their foot apparel and now settled into the long white couch facing the view.

Instinctively, Heather grabbed two of the copper and yellow silk couch-pillows which lay piled in each corner and put them in her lap where she unconsciously traced their edges.

"Okay. Tell me what you know, Heather."

"Arthur won't say anything. He's been quiet and depressed. I've asked him over and over what is going on, but he snaps 'Nothing!' at me, or 'I don't want to talk about it!' That's all he'll answer. But when he says 'I don't want to talk about it', that means there's something to talk about. The 'it' is the problem, whatever 'it' is."

"Do the calls come late at night?"

"Yes, usually between 2 and 3 a.m.; but sometimes on and off until morning. Arthur answers them even though we have an answering machine. I thought that was strange because I'm the one who usually answers the phone when Arthur and I are home. If he's near the phone when it rings, he lets the calls go on the automatic recorder so he can listen to whoever the caller is before answering. But when the calls come late at night, he lunges out of bed and grabs the phone before the message tape begins, so the incoming voice is never recorded. It's as though he's awake waiting and listening for the call because he jumps so quickly, I know he couldn't have been asleep."

"Does he tell you about the call afterwards?"

Heather looked into her lap and fingered the piping at the edge of one copper-colored pillow. "No," she answered quietly.

"And you ask about these night calls?"

Heather snapped her head up, her face blotched from crying. "Yes! I always ask."

A few stray hairs stuck to her cheek from where they had mingled with her sorrow. She brushed these back to rejoin the wavy red mass.

"And?"

"His answer is always the same; 'Business'. If I pry any deeper, he tells me not to worry, that he's handling it. There's that 'it' again. I've begged him to share with me, but he won't. When he comes back to bed after those calls I can feel him staring into the darkness. I can almost hear his mind thinking. He never moves. He'll lay there like a..." she hesitated, shaking her head back and forth, then finished..."like a dead man!" Heather covered her face with her hands as sobs shook her frame. Claire moved to her side putting her arms around Heather. Taking deep breaths to calm herself, Heather looked up and continued, "I thought it might be a woman in the beginning. You can't know how wretched I was, Aunt Claire. One night I crept to the door of Arthur's office and put a glass jar up to it. I read somewhere you can listen through a wall that way. I felt like a fool and would have died from embarrassment if Arthur had found me there. But I had to know if he was seeing another woman."

"Yes, you did. And what did you learn?"

"I knew right away it wasn't a woman. He was talking too rough. I couldn't make out the words, but it was an aggressive unfriendly conversation. I've never heard Arthur so upset. After a few minutes he slammed the phone down so hard I thought it would break. I could hear his breathing through the door. It was like he had been running too hard and was gasping to catch his breath." Heather stared at Claire. "I love Arthur, Aunt Claire. I wanted to go to him then more than I ever have. I couldn't help myself. I knocked on the door and called his name but he told me to go away in a loud angry voice.

"I pleaded with him and even tried the door, but he had locked it. I was frightened, and implored him to let me in. Finally, he flung the door open and when I saw him, I couldn't believe what I saw. He didn't look like Arthur. His face was bright red, the veins on his forehead stood out, and his eyes bulged. When he talked it was like he was hissing. All I could do was stare. He looked like a different person."

"What did he say?"

"It was too ugly, Aunt Claire."

"I have to know what you know if we're to understand this mystery."

"He accused me."

"Of what?"

"Of whatever this thing is that's going on." Heather shook her head. "I can't stand to remember. It wasn't Arthur!" She caught her breath then continued in a broken voice.

"He said if it wasn't for marrying me he never would have done it, whatever that means. What has he done, and why am I to blame?"

"That's the question. When did you say these calls started?"

"About two weeks ago."

"Every night?"

"Yes."

"Tell me more about that note."

"I found it in Arthur's pocket. It was in the jeans he wore yesterday. I felt like a thief going through his pockets but I have a right, even a duty, to know what's happening with my husband!"

"Yes, you do. Where was he yesterday?"

"He was supposed to be at our South Mall store but each time I called, the store manager acted suspicious. He said Arthur had stepped out for a moment or had just left for lunch, or something else that didn't sound true. He said he'd have Arthur call the moment he returned. I was so worried I called every hour anyway, only to be told he was out of the store for one excuse or another. When I asked if Arthur had left a message for me the manager answered 'No' each time. I considered leaving our Main Street store and driving to South Mall but I felt certain Arthur wouldn't be there. Somehow I got through the day and hurried home at 5 p.m."

"Was Arthur there?"

"He was sitting in his office with no lights on. I don't know how long he had been here, but he was wearing his bathrobe. He had his back to the door and was staring at a corner of the ceiling. I tiptoed up to him and kissed the top of his head. He sprang to his feet and spun around to face me. He was furious. He told me never to sneak up on him like that again, then he told me to get out because he had important work to do. He actually took my arm and escorted me, then slammed the door behind me and locked it."

"I stood there frozen, in disbelief, but somehow managed to change clothes and fix a meal. I knocked on his door to tell him dinner was ready, but he answered he wasn't hungry. That's all he said. Of course, I couldn't eat a bite, so I did chores around the house and went to bed at our usual time. I was afraid to go to his office again because I knew he'd be rough toward me. I thought about calling the police or even an ambulance, because I worried he might hurt himself, maybe shoot himself or

119

something crazy like that. It was torture, Aunt Claire.

"Finally, about midnight he crept into bed and I knew talking was impossible by the way he slid into his side, with his back turned to me. I could tell he intended to be separate and alone. I reached over anyway, and stroked his shoulder." A look of profound sadness crossed over Heather's face. "He jerked away like I had bitten him.

"I lay still the rest of the night. Arthur didn't sleep because his breathing was shallow and rapid. He always snores a few minutes when he first falls asleep then breathes deeply with a few splutters during the night, and sometimes he'll smack his lips." Heather smiled wanly, then sobered again. "But he didn't do any of that. The sun comes up around 6 a.m., but Arthur sprang out of bed at 5:30 and said, 'What was that?' in a fierce whisper, then reached for the handgun he keeps in the drawer next to the nightstand. I told him I hadn't heard anything, but he crept out of the bedroom and searched the house anyway. About ten minutes later he came back and said he had to leave early for work. We've never worked on Sundays. It was a conspicuous lie. I knew it was a lie and he knew it was a lie. I begged him to tell me what was wrong." Heather swiped a fresh fall of tears from her cheeks.

"He dressed in work clothes but before he left he walked to my side of the bed and sat down. He just stared at me. It was horrid, Aunt Claire. There was hatred in his eyes. I wanted to scream. Finally, I couldn't stand it any longer and asked him why he was looking at me that way. At first he didn't answer, then he told me all of it had been for me; all of it was because of me he said.

"After that, he hurried away, slamming the front door on his way out. I was in shock. I kept looking at the spot where he had sat on the bed, until I gradually returned to my senses, and tried to piece things together. That's when, in desperation, I went through his pockets and found the note from Georgie Boy. I called you right away even though I knew you weren't home. I had to do something, so I wrote the letter and took it to your house then came back and waited for your call. While I was waiting, Arthur called and said he was sorry and not to worry. He told me he couldn't come home then hung up. I was beside myself, Aunt Claire, so I called you again and that was when you answered; and here we are." Heather gazed hard into Claire's face for several moments. She was obviously hesitating to say what fear lay on her heart. Claire understood, and waited. "If Georgie Boy is a bookie or a mobster or something, that could mean Arthur owes money, and if Georgie Boy is calling him night after night and writing threatening notes, that means..."

"Yes, it does," Claire interrupted, trying not to sound alarmed and to prevent Heather from having to utter the words they both knew suggested homicide.

Heather croaked in a hoarse whisper. "Could they kill Arthur?"

"I doubt it," Claire answered quickly in what she hoped was a convincing tone, "because if they kill him they'll never get their money. But gangsters aren't famous for kindness either. They could break him up first."

"You mean break his arm or leg?"

"Yes. Money debts make ruthless men more ruthless." When Claire saw the horror on Heather's face, she hurried to add, "Do you have any idea how much he owes?"

Heather shook her head.

"Do you know where he was when he called you?"

"I hadn't thought of that!" Heather jumped to her feet and ran from the room. Claire followed, reaching Heather as she was lifting the phone receiver to her ear. She pushed three buttons on the telephone base, then waited. Heather's hand trembled as she held the receiver to her ear, her lips quietly forming the word 'please' over and over. She froze, and a moment later, ventured, "Arthur? Arthur, please answer me." She slumped into the chair beside the phone and clutched the telephone receiver so tightly her knuckles turned white. "Arthur, I'll die if you don't tell me. I'm your wife, I have to know!" Heather paused, in an attitude of desperate clinging. "Please, Arthur, please," she squeaked, between loud sniffing.

"Yes, I promise.

"Yes, I know where the handgun is kept.

"Yes, I can use it if I have to." This was followed by a long silence.

Heather's posture suggested Arthur finally was divulging his awful secret. She bit her lower lip and shut her eyes in what

121

looked like a painful squint as she listened.

"Yes, I'm still here. I need to hear all of it, Arthur. Please tell me everything.

"$50,000.00? By when?

"That's the down payment for Georgie Boy?

"You owe $100,000.00! How did you; never mind, I'm sorry.

"No! Don't hang up, what's done is done, we can't undo that. We'll pay, that's all.

"I don't know how. We just will, somehow." But her firm resolve crumbled. "Arthur, they'll hurt you! They might even kill you!

"I don't care about that; I can take care of myself. Please come home, we need to be together.

"Yes, yes, I know you want to keep me out of it, but I'm in whatever you're in. Arthur, please come home." Heather removed the receiver from her ear and stared at it, then looked at Claire. "He hung up!"

"Where is he?"

"He won't tell me."

"But you called him."

"If I select a three number code, the telephone automatically dials the last number that called here. Arthur's was the last call when he told me he wasn't coming home, and no one called after that. But I don't know what number he's calling from."

"He owes $100,000.00?"

"Yes," Heather whispered, closing her eyes and rapidly shaking her head back and forth as if to shake away the thought.

"And they want $50,000.00?"

Heather nodded 'yes.'

"By when?"

"Two weeks, and the rest of it the following week."

"Or?"

"Or they'll shoot the horse, is what they told Arthur."

"Do you and Arthur have $50,000.00?"

"No, Aunt Claire. We don't have anything. We're so deep in debt, I feel like we owe everyone in town. The florist, the auto financing company, the bank, I never know what to say when they call about past due bills. Arthur handles our money but the bills never get paid."

For several minutes they sat in silence, as the awful realization sifted its individual way through each personality. Heather stared as though in a coma, straight ahead, at nothing but her internal explosions. Claire mumbled various possible solutions, all the while aware that none of them solved anything. They were marooned. There was no light, no hope, there were only stabbing visions that pounced in the dark from behind.

"We've borrowed and mortgaged every last dollar on the house." She glanced at her diamond wedding ring. "How much do you think...?"

Claire cut her off, "At a pawn shop that ring would only bring a fraction of its value and even if they gave a fair retail price it wouldn't begin to be enough."

Heather jerked her arms into the air as though she had just tossed something over her shoulders backwards. "Then what?"

"At the moment I can't think of anything."

"Aunt Claire! I can't let them hurt Arthur. There must be something!"

"We're helpless. We have no choice but to let things take their course."

"Arthur and I could run away."

"These mafia people, if that's what they are, have connections all over the world. I don't know if you can outrun a debt with underworld figures. And if you could, you might not outdistance them for long."

Heather joined her hands loosely in her lap and twirled her thumbs around and around one another. "I know there is a way to help Arthur and keep him safe," she muttered, "I just know there is a way."

Claire didn't answer because she had no answer.

PART TWO

Chapter Twelve

For the first time in Heather's marriage, Arthur wasn't home with her that night. The house was big and hollow and dark and frightening. Her impulse to try again to reach Arthur was too strong, and at 2 a.m. she swung out of bed, wrapped herself in a fuzzy pink housecoat and tiptoed into Arthur's office. The darkness, the night, the aloneness, crushed her. Her sweetheart, the one who called her Turtle, was in danger. Whenever Arthur used the word 'Turtle' in the daytime, he had said it was to remind her that no matter where they were, that meant he loved her. He had smiled when he said it and looked deeply into her eyes with sheer unabashed love. That one little word, 'Turtle', had become Arthur's confirmation of love for her, of his wanting and needing her. But now, everything had gone dangerous and wrong. "Arthur! How can this be real!"

She punched the buttons that would ring back to the last call. On the second ring someone answered. She knew it was Arthur trying to disguise his voice. "Listen to me, Arthur. If you hang up I'll die!" Heather waited, aware only of her pounding heart, her pounding need, her pounding challenge to convince Arthur.

"Go ahead," he answered.

"Arthur, I've been awake thinking about everything, and I know we can come up with the money. Not $50,000.00 or $100,000.00, but something maybe that will appease Georgie Boy. I know the house is mortgaged, but if we sold everything we own, including my wedding ring..."

Arthur's response froze her, "Don't say that! We aren't selling anything. Our things are our things and that's that!"

"I was only going to say even if we did do that, which I know we aren't; we still wouldn't have enough, but..."

"They won't wait for the money. I have to leave the country."

"No!" she screamed. "Arthur, I can't live without you!"

"I don't have a choice," he insisted.

"Then take me with you! Arthur, please! I have to be with you!"

There was silence at Arthur's end of the phone for what seemed an eternity to Heather. "All right, we'll leave together. But we have to get passports and I can't use my name because they may be watching. We'll have to get new identities. That will be your job."

"Anything! Anything!"

"Okay, Turtle. Now listen carefully. I'm giving you the phone number where I'm staying. Don't write it down, memorize it. From now on, only call me from a pay phone or from your aunt's house. I'm not big enough fish for them to wiretap our home or every place connected to me, but I don't know how serious these guys get. $100,000.00 is a lot of money."

Heather shut her eyes and listened to each number, seven in all.

Even though I walk through the shadow of the valley of death, I will fear no evil, for thou art with me.

"Got it?" Arthur asked.

"Yes," Heather sniffed, as tears of relief and joy trickled down her cheeks. This number was her first light in a world gone dark and crazy.

"Hang up, and try the number," Arthur commanded, "It's too important to take a chance."

The phone clicked on Arthur's end and Heather quickly dialed the numbers he had spoken.

"Okay, now listen, Turtle, I have an idea how to get us out of the country."

In spite of the confusion and disbelief in Heather's mind, she listened carefully to every word Arthur said, etching it on her heart, a heart that lived and beat for him alone. She didn't understand what it all meant, but that was okay. What mattered was that Arthur would take her with him. He said they would go to a country where English was spoken since neither of them knew a foreign language. He hadn't decided which country, but there was time for that. For now, they needed passports, quick, and under aliases.

Arthur said she was to go to the cemetery the following morning and he told her what to do once there. "That's all you need to know for now, Turtle, we'll take it one step at a time. Now get back to bed. Is the gun near your side of the bed?"

"Yes, it's right next to me."

"I wish I was there with you."

"Me too."

Heather didn't sleep as she waited for the breaking of dawn. The phone rang periodically throughout the night. She longed to pinch herself awake from this nightmare, this distorted reality which had become her living breathing life. They were a young married couple, working hard at their video stores, overspending and struggling with debt due to extravagant buying. They were like most other young couples, Heather thought. But how many lives are what they appear? Everywhere life is crippled by troubles.

The sun had barely cleared the horizon as Heather rose for the dreaded events of this new day. She dressed in blue jeans and a long yellow sweater. The top of the garment was formed into a turtleneck to protect her neck from the cold. She brushed her hair then lifted the shiny red maze to let it fall on the outside of the sweatshirt and contrast agreeably against the yellow.

Whatever looks came her way today would be inconsequential. Years of long flaming red hair that always brought attention had resulted in her going forth into the world with a private bearing, ignoring people who noticed her. It was habit now and kept her separate from the swirl of human activity. But today if a brass band followed noisily behind her, she would have been deaf to it. She only saw this immense necessity before her and its potential hazards. Everything else was bland and nonexistent next to helping Arthur.

She slipped into her leather flat-heeled boots with their fuzzy interior and arranged her jean pant legs over the top of them. Next, she hurried into Arthur's office and began leafing through the local phonebook for cemeteries. After a brief study, she wrote down an address then replaced the book into its black ebony wood container Arthur had purchased to house their various phone books.

Hesitating a moment, she decided to punch in the numbers which when combined connected her to the reason she breathed. "Good morning, Arthur, I needed to hear your voice."

"Yea, yea, good morning. When are you going?"

She had hoped for something more affectionate. "They aren't open for another hour, but I'm leaving anyway. I'll grab a cup of coffee on the way."

"Good girl. I've called our stores and acted like everything is normal. The managers think I'm home with a bad flu and you're staying home to nurse me. We have to keep the stores up and running so Georgie Boy doesn't think we're skipping town."

Georgie Boy, Heather mused, sounds like a parrot's name, a parrot that sits on the shoulder of Long John Silver and listens to plots of mutiny and murder.

She was at the entrance to Walnut Glen Cemetery as the gates opened. It was a large cemetery. There was a Saint Paul's catholic cemetery nearby, though the clay of Christians lay in every burial ground as the natural leftover once their souls enter eternity.

The area's first graveyard, though kept now only as a historic plot, was situated 15 minutes beyond the city limits sign. There, a band of missionaries and their families had settled long ago and made friends with the Indians, until one day some rebels in the tribe turned against them and slaughtered every man, woman, and child. Years later, after the Indians were quelled; Italians came from Europe and covered the land in viticulture. For over a hundred years, their ancient cuttings and the offspring had produced the elixir of wine. From then until the present, the vineyards had expanded to the edges of the valley floor and began climbing up onto the mountain flanks, staining them with green, yellow, orange and red.

Heather's thoughts, however, didn't linger on history, they fled to immediate matters. Today she could only think of breaking away from the weight of the world that was pressing down on her and Arthur. She drove straight to the cemetery office.

A short lady, round as a barrel, with eyes the color of pale aquamarine, directed her to the 'Angel's Rest' area of the cemetery. Heather drove slowly through the narrow lanes until she arrived at an area where the head-stones and statues were smaller than those punctuating the remainder of the grounds. Here granite gravestones of lambs and angels and baby animals dominated. Dates of when born and when died showed these children barely had time to live. A feeling ran through Heather, a kind of shudder. Walking carefully to avoid placing her foot atop the area where the child had been laid to rest, and moving between plots as she had learned in early life was the respectful manner, Heather nonetheless felt as though she was desecrating these tiny graves with their precious cargo. She realized that in death they would be exploited by her urgent need.

Continuing her search through the headstones, she felt like a grave robber. It was only Arthur's peril that steeled her nerves and eclipsed any hesitation. She began writing names with corresponding dates of little boys who had been born in Arthur's birth year; 1940. Then she did the same for girls that showed they were born in her birth year of 1950.

Heather was glad to leave because she had reaped on this sacred ground with self-wrought immunity. She stopped at the first phone booth she saw and called the seven numbers that put her into conversation with her primary concern on earth.

"Good girl!" Arthur praised. "Now get to county records. We're becoming safer by the hour, Turtle!"

Thirty minutes later, Heather pushed through two tall metal doors and joined a short line of people waiting each with his or her personal mission of obtaining official certificates. It was not agreeable to contemplate that she was probably the only illicit person in this place. Dishonesty stings a nature that strives to do good and which knows the difference between right and wrong. She hoped her guilt and embarrassment did not show.

While waiting her turn, she looked around the room. Marble and vaulted; official and valid; dead and mausoleum-like; were the impressions that sifted through Heather's thinking.

Finally, she faced a short curly-haired woman, with small eyes close together that squinted as though to see or evaluate more closely. "May I help you?" she asked in a nasal tone. Her little eyes seemed to burn through Heather.

"Arthur! Arthur! I'm afraid!" She screamed inside, then proceeded to answer in a voice so calm it surprised even herself. "I would like death certificates for these names, please." Heather pushed a piece of paper forward. She had rewritten the borrowed names and dates from Walnut Glen Cemetery neatly on a blank sheet of paper.

"Let's see," the nasal voice responded, "That's six certificates. Correct?"

"Correct," Heather answered flatly.

"Six?"

Heather's fear was overcome by anger. "That's right!" She answered impatiently.

The tiny-eyed woman stared up at her, out of habit or scrutiny, Heather wasn't sure. She only knew she didn't like this face that seemed to spot some defect in her request. "I'm working on a family tree," she curtly lied, then reminded herself this clerk was paid to replicate official documents and had no business investigating a customer's purpose. She met the beady eyes of the clerk with a glare.

"It will be a few minutes," returned the nasal voice of the woman as she scooped the paper into her hand and disappeared into a back room. Heather's next thoughts were to reflect on her falsehood about the family tree and feel ashamed

She became aware of ticking from a clock on the wall. She looked up and saw a huge wooden box with a glassed-in face within which a Roman numerated clock in black numbers ticked with mindless precision by way of a brass pendulum swinging like a scythe. As the minutes wore on, there was human shuffling behind her in line and some superficial conversation of the gratuitous type. That struck Heather as honest behavior, and she felt convicted in her dishonest intentions because this building was hallowed as governmental and legitimate. The sounds of these visitors were deferential whispers. There is great strength in law. Its power is life and death. These voices respected because beneath them lay fear and awareness of the laws' compelling dominion over every man, woman, and child.

The curly-haired woman returned with six sheets of paper copied from originals in the depths of the room from where she had just ushered. "That's $12.00," she requested nasally.

Heather paid in cash, following Arthur's directions not to leave a paper trail. She felt the oppressive weight leave her as she exited the building.

Back home, she spread the papers on the long ebony coffee table with its brass fittings, that stood in front of the couch, then read the documents. She needed an exact date of birth. The cemetery stones gave years not dates. Deaths were recorded by name, but births were recorded by date, and these death certificates gave the needed birth date.They also contained the birthplace, some few facts about the parents, and the cause of death. These children had died accidentally; by drowning, by falling from swings, by automobiles, by ingesting something poisonous, only one had passed away from illness; pneumonia. It was upsetting to Heather as she reviewed this litany, but she forced herself because Arthur was her first cause. On a sheet of paper she arranged names with their corresponding birth dates and birth places and parents' names.

Arthur told her birth records are filed in the county of birth, and now from these death certificates, Heather could see where the children had been born. At a glance, she realized all six were born locally so she would have easy access to each birth record. Once she had these birth certificates for herself and Arthur, doors for other official documents would open. Arthur said they would have a large pool of aliases to choose from because the children hardly had time to live, let alone move out of the county.

Heather drove back to the records building, hoping the same squinty-eyed, nasal-voiced woman would be involved with another customer so she could approach a different clerk. This time, she pulled a soft blue cashmere hat over her head to conceal her red hair completely. She also donned dark sunglasses. She reasoned these precautions might keep her from being spotted as a second time visitor in the same day. It never occurred to her that an innocent person could show up a hundred times a day with impunity, while the guilty slink and run even when they are not being chased.

She made an effort to put forth her most relaxed, good-natured, demeanor. A wave of thankfulness swept through her as a skinny hump-nosed young woman with short brown hair indicated Heather was next. The earlier clerk hadn't noticed or recognized her, but Heather kept her body turned away from the neighboring squinty-eyed woman with the nasal voice. The wait for the records was longer this time. Heather heard the clock again and for some reason it sounded louder than her earlier visit. As danger presses in upon the feral animal, its senses quicken. The ears alert and hear better, the nose lifts and smells possible danger, then readies the body to fight or flee. Finally, the hump-nosed girl returned with six sheets of paper, in the now familiar heavy black reproduction. "$12.00," came the request, and Heather once again paid in cash and hastened from the building.

Back home, seated at the couch, she spread the papers onto the table.

The three boys, born in 1940, were Randy McKinney; Samuel Epstein; and Carl Larsen. The girls, whose birth year was 1950, read Suzanne Embers; Eve Harrington; and Sally Miller.

Carefully sliding the six papers into Arthur's eel skin binder, Heather left the house and drove to the pay phone she now used exclusively to contact Arthur. She chose this spot because it was located at a far corner of a gas station property and afforded privacy. Across the street was a fire department. As she dialed the precious numbers to reach Arthur, she could see men inside the building. They were cleaning their red fire trucks while engaged in what appeared to be friendly conversation. Envy pervaded her thoughts as she realized the legitimacy of their work. Something about its honesty made her yearn for the everyday world that now seemed forever separate from these furtive criminal motives and movements of hers. She felt despair over her lack of decency and for a moment, just before finishing the numbers, she hesitated because she felt an overwhelming longing to return to the common kind of day. Then she completed the dialing, and continued along her reckless course. Under all she did now was a jungle beat. Behind the thick vegetation with its ponderous leaves, somewhere in that tangled other world she heard a distant drumming upon stretched skin, like a heartbeat growing louder and faster. She felt danger from a predator. Her scent was blood wafted on the air.

"Yes?"

"Hi. You have three choices. Do you want to be Randy, Samuel, or Carl?"

A moment of hesitation followed before Arthur answered. "Randy. Where was I born and who are my parents?"

"You were born at Walnut Glen General on December 15th, 1940. Your full name is Randy Lee McKinney. Your parents are Lillian Margaret McKinney and Frank Lee McKinney. Your birth took place at 11:07 a.m., and your birth weight was 7 pounds, 3 ounces. There were no complications at birth and the presiding doctor was David Abrams."

"And you?" Arthur asked.

"I am Suzanne Joyce Embers, born August 25th, 1950 at the same hospital. My parents are Amelia Diane Embers and John Everet Embers. I was born at 9:03 a.m. and weighed 10 pounds, 3 ounces. The doctor made a note regarding difficult labor. The doctor's name was Christian Wesley." Heather took a deep breath. "Now what?"

She laid the certificates on the cold metal shelf inside the phone booth and glanced down the quiet residential street that stretched until disappearing as one diminishing line. The huge-trunked trees along the street told how established the neighborhood was. The leaves were golden and orange and red. Their coloring continued as a strewn palette onto the lawns and sidewalks and into the street. Heather could see the leaf stems sticking up which gave the appearance of tiny-masted becalmed skiffs. The bright red ones looked like Maraschino cherry stems above fruit flattened into leaf shape. Arthur broke her musings, but not before she had a pull, an unmistakable yearning, to skip down that street and never look back.

"We have to meet somewhere tomorrow."

The thought of seeing Arthur snapped her attention back to the moment. "Arthur! Thank goodness! Where? When?"

"We'll need driver's licenses next, Turtle. The only document we need for that is a birth certificate."

Heather was confused. "Why do we need..."

He cut her short. "Are you with me or aren't you?" It was a hostile retort and Heather couldn't stand its potential.

"Of course I'm with you."

"Okay, then trust me. We have to leave the country, right?"

"Right."

"You can't get a passport without several I.D. pieces, and that's what we're doing, we're getting I.D.s, one at a time."

"I understand, Arthur, I'm sorry."

He blew out a deep breath, like steam squeezing through a tight fitting lid atop boiling water. "Turtle, I know this is hard on you. It's hard on me too. But we'll be together again and everything will be great. We'll find a nice country. Australia I've been thinking would be a good choice. Think about us together in a sunny country with a new start." His words dispelled her gloom. How she needed him; his reassurance, his direction. "Okay?" he finished.

"Yes," she answered firmly.

"Tomorrow at 8:30 a.m. meet me at the southeast corner of the parking lot at the Department of Motor Vehicles. Bring Randy's and Suzanne's' birth certificates and I'll tell you then how to go about the driving test. And Heather?"

"Yes, Arthur?"

"Rent a car and cruise around for a while to make sure you're not being followed."

"I will."

"Tomorrow then, Turtle, my love."

Heather heard a click from Arthur's end of the line. She removed the receiver from her ear and stared at it. Arthur was in there somewhere and their plight was real. She wondered what other grim plans had gone through this black metal device of a telephone in the Plexiglas surround with gouged messages from disordered thoughts and feelings.

She didn't sleep well that night. Her body continually switched between sweating and chills.

The phone rang every hour. The answering machine recorded the same thing over and over. It was deep coarse breathing and gum-chewing, then a click when the caller hung up. Heather knew it was Georgie Boy and part of the underworld's terror as it toyed with its victim before the kill.

She remembered grisly films of nature shown on television, of the cheetah and how the mother was weakened after giving birth and had to seek a young gazelle for food because they were a less strenuous catch. The mother cat spotted her food, and as the intended baby gazelle ran its wobbly-legged way, it couldn't outrun the cheetah, not even an exhausted one. But how it ran, with all its tiny might, with fear and shock, and blind instinct to live. The cheetah wasn't content to kill quickly. She enjoyed the hunt and played with and taunted her victim, rolling it over for its new legs to thrash the air before righting itself then desperately running, even dragging itself to get away. The baby creature didn't know it was doomed. The cat would let it gain some distance in false hope, then spring at it again, crippling it more and more each time. Finally, the cheetah grasped its throat and the young gazelle bleated its final sound.

That pattern of life needing death to sustain life seemed cruel in its necessity. It was enigmatic and mysterious. Always in those horrid pictorials she would look away from the sacrifice of one life given to uphold another. She knew even in Christianity this pattern was true. Jesus Christ offered his life so others could live eternally through his sacrifice that paid for our sins. Dark mysteries, thought Heather; deep, unfathomable truths.

This night, she wouldn't have slept even if there had been no calls. She wanted to turn off the phone altogether, but Arthur said to leave it connected and note what activity Georgie Boy was generating. He thought he could monitor the danger that way. As instructed, she had the handgun by her side all night, but Arthur was certain Georgie Boy and his underworld friends knew he was gone from the home. Until Arthur's deadline passed without receiving their money, he assured Heather they wouldn't harm anyone. Once they knew Arthur couldn't pay, things could change. Then their criminal natures might surface. Then they would be capable of anything to get what they wanted.

By 8 a.m. she was at the southeast corner of the parking lot. The car rental had gone smoothly. The twisting route she had taken proved no one was tagging her, so now Heather sat anxiously awaiting the man she had vowed to love through good times and bad times. She didn't have long to wait. At 8:15, Arthur appeared from the edge of the large parking lot, already filled at this early hour. For a moment Heather wasn't certain it was Arthur. He had bleached his hair and cut it short against his scalp, like stubble. He wore dark sun glasses, but not so dark as to appear furtive.

In spite of the lateness in the year, today the sky was open blue with big puffy clouds scudding along like white tugboats. The air was brisk and there was dampness everywhere from recent rains. Heather's heart began to pound as Arthur reached for the handle on the passenger side of her car and climbed in.

Their embrace was immediate and fierce.

"Turtle, Turtle, Turtle," he repeated into her ear.

Heather responded with a quivering body and sobs. How could this be, this regular normal effort to live, to be a married young couple, with businesses of their own, and a home, and with a longing, at least in her heart, to begin a family and fill the house with joyous sounds from their children. No, here they were instead; paranoid, frightened, and pulling lies into their daily existence as though harvesting a ripe evilness unto themselves, as Adam and Eve ate the forbidden fruit and brought sin into the world.

These and other thoughts flew through Heather's thinking, then she felt Arthur's lips on hers and everything dissolved but this nearness to him, and his soft hungry pressure upon her mouth. She responded with a need that equaled his. Finally, they broke their embrace and looked long and hard into each other's eyes. Arthur swiped the tears from her cheeks.

"Nothing has looked so good to me in a long time, Turtle. It seems like forever since I've held you."

"It feels that way to me too. So many things have happened since we were together. It's torture being without you."

Arthur was stroking her hair and kissing the top of her head. "I never knew there was so much red in the world until I couldn't be around you and everything red reminded me of you." He sighed deeply. "Okay, let's get down to business. We can't lose track of what's going on here. Let me see the birth certificates."

Heather reached into the back and lifted the eel-skin folder from the seat. From inside the container she produced two documents. She handed one to Arthur.

Nervously, he scanned the paper, then murmured, "Randy Lee McKinney, mother's name Lillian Margaret McKinney; maiden name, O'Keefe. Father's name Frank Lee McKinney. I was born 12/15/40 here in Walnut Glen at Walnut Glen General.

All right. Now let's both memorize the information in case anyone asks the basic questions at a point when we aren't holding these birth certificates up to our noses."

They proceeded to commit to memory their chosen aliases, then quizzed one another. "Suzanne Joyce Embers, born 8/25/50, at Walnut Glen General. My mother's name is Amelia Diane Embers; maiden name, LeVeque. My father is John Everet Embers."

These stolen identities were repeated several times, then Arthur brushed Heather's' hair from her forehead and kissed her repeatedly above her eyes. She let this shower of affection comfort her, and realized she had become a weary terrified soul.

"Ready, Turtle?" he asked.

She nodded her head in a 'yes' motion.

"I'll go first. You wait a few minutes then come in. Remember; act as though you don't know me. I'll use the car I rented when they do the road test, and you use this one. Afterwards, go to the phone booth and call so we can compare notes."

With that, Arthur swung out of the car and headed toward the entrance of the Department of Motor Vehicles with the required birth certificate in his hand. For an instant, Heather saw the paper as a white flag of truce in this darkness squeezing them painfully toward a slow death. The white flutter Arthur grasped was the warmth; a new land together; sandy beaches; freedom and sunlight; compared to this furtive hole.

Heather pulled the rearview mirror to arrange her hair and apply fresh lipstick. It was again a time she was reminded how she stood out with her mass of red hair when she wanted to be invisible. She slipped on her sunglasses and opened the car door.

"You've never had a driver's license?" the clerk asked, after an uneasy wait that had seemed to go backwards in time when she needed to go forward at the speed of light and faster than the speed of light.

"No. My husband has always driven me."

The clerk, a young Mexican woman with black hair pulled into a bun and eyebrows penciled in thin black lines above her natural brow-line that had been plucked or shaven or somehow removed, answered, "My mother was the same way. She never wanted to learn."

Heather felt the pressure lift from her body at these words. She thanked providence for guiding her to this window where the notion of an American beyond the age of 16 without a driver's license was tantamount to disbelief.

It was quickly perceived that memorizing the birth certificate's details was a critical asset because the high-browed girl now asked Heather particulars in a confirming sort of way as she filled out the paperwork, but in so doing caused the document to be upside down to Heather's view. "Suzanne Joyce Embers, and your birth date, Suzanne?" the woman asked, scanning the document.

"August 25th, 1950," Heather answered quickly.

"Born where?" Again, the clerk perused the paper.

Heather answered from memory through additional questions. It must have been only five minutes but the time squeezed against her and caused everything to distort. There was clashing in her mind between readiness to respond with a lie, and panic urging her to turn and run away as fast as she could. All the while, the horrible awareness that she was actually doing this thing, that she was in fact pursuing a false identity, and lying to this sweet polite woman made her feel like the forked tongue of a snake.

The woman handed her the birth certificate clipped to various other papers then pointed toward a bench across the huge room. "You can wait over there. A driving instructor will be with you as soon as possible."

Heather offered a brief "thank you" as she left the window. She wiped the perspiration from the sides of her nose and from her forehead then veered outside for some fresh air and a few moments to compose herself before the next step.

Re-entering, she sat on the bench the high-browed woman had indicated. She was third in line. Arthur was first. This sham was surreal and hateful; sitting here as Suzanne Joyce Embers, and her husband as Randy Lee McKinney, dishonestly playing their roles of not knowing each other. There were people she had read about who enjoyed this sort of intrigue. They would meet somewhere, maybe in a bar, and act like they were strangers then go home together as though it was the first time they had met, even though they were married over 25 years and living together in the same house. Now, she and Arthur added to the endless arrangements of unnatural behavior. She longed to be whom and what she was; she longed to be Heather Bainbridge Conway, a regular girl trying to be good and moral. But here she was; in Satan's court.

Arthur was summoned and disappeared through the door and out of sight behind a man carrying a clipboard. Ten minutes later a woman, also with a clipboard, called the next person, and Heather moved to the #1 position. Her anxiety mounted with each passing minute. She tried to steady her mind that fidgeted between her inner self and the surface persona of Suzanne Joyce Embers. You are already discovered. We know each pattern. You cannot change what is fixed.

The man who had summoned Arthur, was soon guiding her into the busy street as she drove the rented vehicle and seemed perfectly unaware she was anyone but Suzanne Embers. She was too intent trying to look awkward at driving to worry about her identity. Remembering what Arthur had told her, she intentionally drove in a jerking nervous way since this was supposed to be her first time to obtain a license.

The examiner yelled, "Look out!" and grabbed various parts of the interior for support and defense within the vehicle. Heather had tried so hard to drive poorly she nearly crashed into another car at an intersection. She was supposed to yield to the car on the right and failed to do so. After several concluding maneuverings onto the freeway and through a school district, the man directed her back to the Department of Motor Vehicles. He sat in the passenger seat for several minutes writing on his paper attached to the clipboard. "That was a very close call at the intersection, Suzanne. You almost didn't pass because of it."

"It's only because I'm nervous about being tested. I'm really a very good driver."

He stopped writing and looked at her in a questioning way. "In spite of that mistake, it's hard to believe you've never had a driver's license."

She didn't respond, but knew she had to. Words began to form for answer, but the examiner was out of the car before she could give an explanation. She was glad to have been spared another lie; lies piling high enough to reach dew point on the flat-bottomed cumulus clouds above her. Every movement of her life felt untrue and deceiving.

The photo for the license was taken and she signed her first official document with the alias of Suzanne Joyce Embers. The clerk handed her a temporary license, adding, "Your license will be mailed in two weeks."

Leaving the building Heather drove immediately to the phone booth across from the fire station and called Arthur. Along the way she wondered about the driving instructor's comment that it was hard to believe she had never held a driver's license and what's worse, she worried that she wasn't convincing. If her alias was that easy to see through they may not make it safely out of the country. She had never been good at acting. She was too shy for anything of the sort. But something had translated amiss to the instructor, she was sure of that. He probably didn't believe her and expressed his doubt, perhaps saving face from being thought to be duped.

Arthur told her not to worry. "He's not a detective, he gives driving tests. There's no need to think twice about it, Turtle."

Chapter Thirteen

The dark circles under Heather's eyes looked to her like they were permanent. Claire noticed them too. It was a Wednesday afternoon. One week had passed since the driving test. Heather talked with her Aunt briefly each day on the phone, but they didn't speak about Arthur's situation for fear of a wiretap. At lunch Heather spoke freely.

"If I couldn't talk to you, Aunt Claire, I would go crazy."

"Well, you can talk to me, so you won't go crazy."

"The waiting is torture. What happened that I ended up here?"

"I think it's called falling in love, and I will probably overstep my boundaries to add; perhaps falling in love with the wrong man?"

"Arthur is the right man! This is just a little trouble he got into. It could have happened to anyone." She knew she sounded desperate.

Claire scanned the face of her lovely redheaded niece sadly, noticing again the dark circles under her eyes. She decided to pursue her outspoken thought because she was fearful for Heather's safety. "I think it's on the rare, sensational side to outrun a mobster, or whoever they are, in order to save your life. Why don't you stay and start over? You aren't in danger. You could move in with me and begin nurse's training. We could have coffee at our sunny breakfast table like before, and this agony would be gone from your life."

Claire waited, studying her niece's countenance then offered softly, "You are at a crossroads, Heather. Your husband is running for his life from a heavy debt owed to shady people. Assuming false identities, like you are doing, is a crime. Even if you hide in a foreign country you will always feel like a hunted animal. It will stay that way for as long as you live dishonestly. You will never stop looking over your shoulder. You will always feel dirty inside to begin every friendship with a lie. You will never like yourself, and eventually you won't like Arthur either. The only way to fix the situation you're in is to face it and change it. You have to make it right."

Heather's voice was incredulous. "But that could mean Arthur's death!"

Claire chose to ignore this outburst. "You have a chance to follow your dream. All your life, you have had a tender compassionate nature, like your mother. Remember the splint you put on the robin with the broken leg when you were a little girl and the joy we both felt the day you released the bird after it healed? And that little turtle you called Tiptoe? It fell down the heat register and cracked its shell. You said you would fix its 'roof' and you did."

Heather smiled. "Yes, I remember. I mixed fresh mud every couple of days and patched it over the crack. Tiptoe looked funny for a while, but after a month I stopped treatments because the shell was repaired. It was sweet, wasn't it, Aunt Claire?" Heather picked up her spoon and began fingering it nervously.

Claire knew the activity of Heather's mind needed to overflow by her toying of fingers. She knew there was much over which Heather was nervous and distraught and Claire wouldn't have minded if Heather had needed even to shred the tablecloth little piece by little piece. Releasing the spoon, Heather lifted her palms upward. That little movement told Claire that Heather's heart had won.

"I love him. If I abandoned him in his hour of need I wouldn't be any kind of wife or person."

"There are the laws of the heart," Claire responded, "and there are the laws of the land, and there are the laws of God. Is your decision within each of these?"

Heather tightened her lips and fingered again the metal spoon before speaking. "The first; yes. The second; no. And the third? I don't know how God sees this. I know marriage is forever; through all adversity. How could God not agree I should be with Arthur through this?"

"I remember an expression that goes, 'God is Light and in Him is no darkness at all.' I see assuming false identities and escaping to Australia as darkness."

"I don't know what I think or feel anymore," Heather

answered in a low bitter voice. It was a tone Claire had never heard from her sunny-visage niece. "I've never felt this way in my life. I didn't think it was possible to be involved with something so ugly." Heather slapped the spoon down onto the tablecloth and blew out a slow breath. "I'm going with him, Aunt Claire. If I didn't, I would always wonder if I made the wrong decision. This way I'll know. I'll try to get my husband through this and if we fail..." she paused, a look of panic swiftly crossing over her face. "If we fail," she repeated softly, "I can always know I did all I could possibly do." Heather looked into her aunt's face. "Aunt Claire, I love my husband, and I love you. Please try to understand my predicament. You're right, I've always dreamed of nursing school." Heather laughed. "That seems like another universe compared to my life now!" Then sobering, she concluded, "I need your support, Aunt Claire. I can't stand it if you hate me."

"Don't say that! Don't ever even think that!" Claire reached over and with both hands cupped Heather's cheeks. "I love you, and I will be your Aunt Claire through thick and thin." Heather's eyes misted over. In her ears she heard her heart beating fast and hard. This unconditional love from her aunt was the life vest that kept her from drowning.

Two weeks of waiting was a lifetime every day. The hours were a tonnage on her shoulders. Arthur's time to pay was up. The unknown was now dangerous. Existence felt like a dizzy precipice along which she balanced. She was hyper alert even though she functioned in what on the surface pretended to be a calm manner.

First, the dogs barked down at the start of her block and proceeded in a continuous pattern from dog to dog along the street, heralding the arrival of the postman. Each day, Heather hid behind the drawn blinds of her window and peeked until she saw the swarthy pig-tailed man with his postal bag lugged upon his shoulder, fingering items of mail for the final selection of what was to become her's and Arthur's delivery.

Arthur had said using the same address for their driver's licenses to be sent wouldn't pose a hazard. Government computers didn't list driver's licenses by addresses and even if they did, two different people at one address wasn't illegal, unless a sharp detective's eye wondered how two adults at the same address suddenly applied for first time licenses. But that wouldn't happen Arthur swore to her, then accused her of being paranoid. It stung Heather to hear this harsh reprimand from him. Though later, alone in the darkness of that night, she decided his scolding stopped her from a panicked run; a blind breaking of rank and running off wildly in any direction.

She peeped out the window again and noted the pig-tailed man had already delivered their mail and was arranging the paper deposit for their neighbor. Heather waited until he was out of sight before opening the door, then hastily emerged and collected the mail. The thought of Georgie Boy made her actions clandestine, and this sneaky behavior made even her most innocent actions feel criminal.

The sensation of scrutinizing her picture on a driver's license with the name Suzanne Joyce Embers, and then to see Arthur's, and his name as Randy Lee McKinney, was a mocking sting to Heather. "I'm not hurting anyone," she repeated, as she had what seemed a thousand times each day. Could she factually believe this rationalization from a tiny voice within? She couldn't and she knew she couldn't, but regardless of that she chose the lie in order to be with Arthur. He was all that mattered in every decision she made.

She proceeded into the bedroom and pulled on a pair of lined black wool slacks, a green sweater and low-heeled black zip-up boots. She stuffed her red hair under a black head-hugging wool hat and put on dark glasses.

Careful as always to maneuver through a residential area to make sure she wasn't being followed, Heather drove to the familiar phone booth across from the fire station. She saw the men inside the firehouse and for a wild moment wondered how it would be to marry a fireman. The idea was pleasant even knowing no one could outdo her love for Arthur.

"It's about time they arrived!" Whatever Arthur said was the sound that healed a part of her brokenness.

They arranged a meeting place, the outer edge of a busy grocery store parking lot. Again their embrace was furious and clinging. Finally, Arthur broke their connection. "Now listen," he said, "Tomorrow we apply for a social security number. I'll manage some story about myself, but for you it will be a snap since lots of females don't work their entire lives. You've decided to try a job, which is all you have to say. Got it?"

She nodded her head up and down, and then searched Arthur's face as if she was seeing it for the first time. His skin was drawn and Heather noticed that worry wrinkles had appeared between his eyebrows. "I can already smell the Eucalyptus trees," she offered in an attempt to cheer the gloomy spell over their lives.

"Yea, yea, so call after you get the number. I'll go when they open. You go late in the afternoon so it won't draw attention that two first time social security numbers are being issued the same day. Just in case. Okay?"

The process was smooth. The clerk was cheerful about helping Heather, and even congratulated her. "Good luck, Suzanne. I wish you success in the working world. It can be very rewarding."

Heather felt fully deceptive compared to this woman's sincerity, and it stung deeply into her nature. But she and Arthur were finally set, and that precluded all things under the sun. They had a birth certificate, a driver's license, and a social security number under their assumed names. Finally, they could proceed with the final and long-awaited paper that would take them to freedom; the coveted passport.

These false visits to conduct bureaucratic business were becoming easier for Heather. She was gradually learning to be dishonest in a more relaxed way. Yet, it was futile to ignore her disgust at herself as the dishonesty multiplied.

The day she drove to the federal building, it was storming. Rain poured like cataracts from the sky. Vehicles had their lights on in the darkness of the day and windshield wipers sped back and forth struggling to keep up with the flood of rain.

Heather realized this process had a different feel to it. She determined it was because this was an immense federal building. There was something thicker about the walls and higher about the ceilings and more serious about the clerks. She was practiced enough now, however, to act the part of Suzanne Embers and it was only an hour later she had made her application and paid her fees out of the new checking account she had opened as Suzanne

Embers. In fact, this was the first check she had written under her new name.Back in her car driving home through the rain, she stopped at the phone booth contact point and learned that Arthur also had an easy time of it. Now they only needed to wait the required processing time. Two weeks and they would have their passports and disappear forever together.

This was the only time since their decision to leave that Heather felt close to normal. The maze of lies and deceptions had born bleakness that filled her being. But at last, and despite the utter lack of truthful behavior, Heather felt sure that she and the man she loved beyond measuring would be together again, with no threats of harm hanging over them day and night.

It was 13 days since she applied for her false passport. Heather knew the exact minute it changed into one more day's worth of waiting.

The restaurant Claire, Rose, and Heather entered was half-filled with customers. They were lead to a corner padded booth under a long bank of mirrors. "The beef medallions are excellent," Rose offered, "that's my choice." She snapped the menu shut and leaned back. Heather had the same, while Claire opted for Caesar's salad. They all chose a bowl of minestrone soup; mixed fruit; and a glass of Chardonnay.

It was difficult for Heather to pay attention to the conversation because of the tumultuous sensations running through her. In another week she would be gone forever, and she might never see these beloved faces of Aunt Claire and Rose again. Both were loved by her since childhood. Fighting not to become sentimental and break down in tears, she struggled to remain detached from this close, and perhaps final, gathering.

Rose watched Heather intensely, and finally addressed her aloofness. "What are you thinking about so diligently, young lady?"

"Nothing in particular, Rose."

"What you mean is you don't want to talk about it," Rose answered in her frank, but friendly way.

Heather grinned in return, and saw Rose's heart-shaped smiling cupid mouth and the twinkle in her eyes. She felt like gushing forth with a full confession of the horrible gale beating against her. But how could she? Even to this life-long friend, how could she? It was painful to be shut in alone with guilt. "Maybe sometime later, Rose. Right now, I can't talk about it."

My mouth is duct-taped because I belong to a crime scene. I am roped off from the crowd. I am yellow tape. My blood doesn't fit and wants to go against itself and get out, even as it clings to the treachery, even as evidence claims it.

"A stitch in time," Rose quipped.

"I know, but I can't."

Rose folded her arms across her chest and thoroughly scrutinized Heather. Then she unfolded the clutch and turned her attention onto Claire. The rest of their luncheon was friendly conversation without touching upon serious matters.

"Why are they taking so long?" Heather pleaded into the phone on her nightly call to Arthur. "It's been over three weeks."

"Call them tomorrow," Arthur concluded.

"Suzanne Embers, Suzanne Embers..." the man at the receiving end of the phone at the passport office repeated absentmindedly, followed by silence. "Yes, here we are. It's ready. You can come in and pick it up whenever you like."

"Can't you mail it to me?"

"No, Ma'am. Passports can't go out in the mail."

"I'll be in later today. Thank you."

Heather hurried to the phone across from the fire station. "It's here! At least mine is which means yours should be too. Take this phone booth number. I'll wait for you to check on yours and then call me back."

Within a few minutes Arthur rang back. "Are you packed, Turtle?"

Heather made a joyful squeal, then hastened to add, "I've been packed for weeks."

"Not too much, I hope?"

"No, I was careful. I brought five changes of clothes, my favorite picture of Aunt Claire, some of our wedding picture, a few personal items like cosmetics and perfume, and of course, my rock."

"Your what?"

"My rock."

"Okay, I give. What do you mean, 'my rock'?"

"Arthur!"

"Randy," he corrected.

"Randy," she continued, "it's from the first time we went shopping together. We stopped in a gem store and I saw a sparkling stone from Russia called a Celestite. It has long crystals growing out of a blue surface. You bought it for me even though the price was high. You don't remember?"

"Vaguely. How much does it weigh?"

Heather felt a sharp disappointment. "Not very much, why?"

"Our weight is limited. We can only bring essentials."

"Arthur, my rock is essential!"

"Okay, okay, but no other frills, and it's Randy."

Back home, Heather carefully selected her clothing. Today, Friday, marked the beginning of a new life, or at least the brink to that beginning. She chose to wear her wool slacks in silver gray that were lined top to bottom in a slippery coolness that was pleasant against her delicate skin and protected her from the scratchiness of wool. For a sweater, she pulled her favorite one from the closet, a black knit from Italy with a mandarin collar and long sleeves. Off to one side of the high-standing neck was a vertical slit. At the top of that was a bow of the same fabric as the sweater. The gap was closed by two large crystal buttons, giving a strong feminine glitter to sparkle from that side of her neck. She chose her Italian black leather shoes, then wound a soft, black and charcoal patterned muffler around her neck and let the ends fall to either side down the front, then slipped into her long black wool coat.

The drive into the city was an odd mixture for Heather. Part of her was calm, for at last the long awaited papers had arrived and all her's and Arthur's frantic efforts would be realized. Another part of her was, as usual, dismayed to be going about the business of an illegal identity. She consoled herself by concluding that this document would be the last in the series they needed. One more time of cheating and that would be the end of it. Arthur had told her eventually they would switch back to their real names but it wouldn't be for about ten years. Heather held to that distant hope.

She found an easy parking space and plugged the meter with several dimes. Before entering the federal building she glanced at the clear cold sky above the city. Its blue canvas was decorated with white clouds like taffy pulls. She hesitated, in a quick study of one particular cloud pattern. On closer inspection, its appearance was like that of an angel, with wings fanned out, the tips curving upward and a head leaned back. There was even an expression on the face she saw there. It was a fantastic face as only clouds can be, and seemed to be supplicating to something higher than itself. The body was robed and flowing, first solid, then gauze-like toward the end, after which it trailed into invisibility and the blue sky dominated again. Heather felt soothed by the angel cloud above her in its posture of praying.

She pushed through the thick-glassed front doors of the federal building and followed the signs to the passport desk. There was no one else waiting in line so Heather approached a lean young bald man behind the counter. "My name is Suzanne Embers, I'm here to pick up my passport," she stated calmly.

The man nodded and began to thumb through several piles, while repeating the name, "Suzanne Embers, Suzanne Embers." He extracted one sheet from the rest and read it silently. "Here we are, Suzanne. Yes, I'll get your passport. Wait here, I'll just be a moment."

Five minutes later, Heather was still waiting patiently. She later reflected about the following moments, maybe even as often as ten thousand times it eventually ran through her thinking. Something came from behind, a voice, two voices, but before that, a feeling, a thrust and assertion around her. The voice over her left shoulder inquired, "Suzanne Embers?"

"Yes," she responded without turning. It happened fast. The first visible connection was an arm from the right side positioning something at eye level in front of her face. It was similar to a woman's compact mirror, except it had a man's picture on it. All Heather recognized were three bold letters: FBI.

The voice attached to the arm holding this unprecedented statement of authority asked, "May we go upstairs? We'd like to ask you a few questions."

Heather couldn't speak. She could only nod dumbly. Reality was dark and muggy inside this tight cocoon that suddenly blinded and muffled her. Somehow, she was standing in front of an elevator, an FBI agent on either side. Once they stepped inside that chamber, Heather found her voice. There were no other passengers. Tears sprang from her eyes as she spoke. "I'm not a criminal. I want to be a nurse someday." She was misery. She was broken because she was tender.

The two men were unmoved as she trembled throughout her body. She opened her purse to find her handkerchief, but one agent immediately grabbed her purse. "May I help you find something, Ma'am?"

For the first time, Heather looked into the face of the FBI agent who had just spoken. His voice wasn't harsh. He even had a mild pleasant face. She squeaked, "I need my handkerchief."

I am Helium. Let loose my string. I am strangled. Release my captivity so that I may rise. Let my breath mingle with the clouds and their honesty.

"Yes, Ma'am, I'll get it for you".

"It's yellow," she rasped between sobs.

He handed her the yellow cloth then zipped the purse together and kept it.

Heather froze, trying to make big thoughts fit through tiny passages; trying to walk on newly amputated feet. Only her eyes moved between the man's face and her purse. Her puzzlement was obvious because he answered, "Sorry, Ma'am, we have to check this in."

It felt like a part of her had been torn off. She was Venus di Milo. Her shock began to spin the surroundings and she wasn't sure she would keep consciousness. The kind-faced man holding her purse spoke, "Are you okay, Ma'am?" Then he made a confession, "This is the first time I've arrested a woman."

She mumbled something in response but didn't know what because his word 'arrested' was ripping through her. Arrested! Arrested! Heather repeated in her mind. Aunt Claire's niece? Arrested? Rose's friend? Arrested? Arthur's wife? Arrested? A girl made to help others? Arrested? It sped by her in a blur. Only later would she be able to face and endure this shock. For now, she was removed from herself and watching from a distance as a crucifixion proceeded against someone with red hair, visibly shaking, and sputtering words that claimed she was good.

She was led to a desk behind which a huge man with a coarse manner ruled. He took her purse from the FBI agent and turned it upside down, spilling the contents over the counter.

Heather felt naked. His gesture disrobed her. Her private feminine life lay exposed to these three strange men. She was dumped like garbage into a heap and handled roughly as the man pushed his hairy hands through her delicate items. Up for inspection went the diamond to the Gorilla's face before he tossed it away.

Instinctively, Heather made a gesture toward her things, but the man pushed her hand away. Stunned by his deflection, she shifted her attention onto his face.

Impatience and disgust rose high across his bearing toward her. Throughout her adult life, this hard reaction from another human being was an experience Heather would always remember. How ugly was the contempt this stranger felt for her and the utter disrespect he exhibited by fiercely knocking her delicate belongings around in his search. It was not caring. Worse, it was hatred.

Heather knew if she had dropped dead right then, he would have made a comment about the inconvenience, then proceeded with his work. Even in her current state of confusion and fright, Heather knew this man was dulled in all sympathetic human ways, as when one is lost in a snowstorm and begins to freeze. First there is the numbing at the extremities, the fingers and toes, before it travels inward along the limbs toward the main trunk of the body where the heart and life abide. The brain fights its fight for the organism's life, eliminating everything under its control in order to keep the heart beating. But the cold keeps coming until all is gone but the brain and the heart. Then the brain shuts down, heroically sacrificing itself to the heart. That was the deadness of this man across from her making an inventory of her articles. He was a hungry raccoon pawing over an elegantly set dinner table. He was jaded beyond repair except for the one Door he would never open.

There was her hair brush with its few red hairs from this morning's combing stuck in the bristles, and her yellow note pad with the Panda bear decoration from a stationary-set Arthur had brought home to her as a cheerful gift when she suffered her last cold. Her little bottle of Christian Dior perfume lay on its side, nestled next to her lipstick case with its small elongated rectangular mirror inside to help guide lipstick over lips needing a color freshening. The coarse man opened this case and dumped out the lipstick tube. It landed with a clanking sound, then rolled and joined her personal life scattered and piled atop this counter.

Next, he opened her wallet and shook its contents onto the other items. Coins and papers and money bills and pictures landed onto the heap. The man held her wallet above his head, fanning wide all its recesses to catch any reluctant resident. Satisfied that all had been mustered, he tossed the wallet, like a broken body, on top of the other items, then made a few notes on a piece of paper. Heather continued to stare in amazement at her precious connections with daily personal life strewn so crudely. The man opened her purse like a yawning pit and in one movement swept everything into it.

Somehow she expected that now, finally, he would hand her purse over to her, even in its violated condition. Instead, he took several steps in the opposite direction and deposited it on a shelf. He gave one of the detectives a paper regarding her purse. Next he reached under the counter and pulled out a plastic bracelet. He wrote the words "felony passport" on a thin piece of paper and slipped it inside the see-through bracelet. After this, he turned then turned and hurried away without a word, quiet and satisfied from the fresh kill.

The remaining process was looking through a squeezing atmosphere. Her picture was taken while she held a numbered plaque under her chin, then there was a profile photo.

The photographer wouldn't answer when she made a desperate attempt to be civilized. She spoke from despair. She needed humane feelings. She needed hope in this maelstrom sucking her down. He responded with blunt rude directions on how to position her head and moved the sign into place with a roughness that caused bruises to emerge later under her chin.

The man who took her fingerprints was angry because her shaking fingers caused smudging. He pushed her finger-ends harder the second time, until she nearly cried out in pain.

Then she was alone with a huge black woman who wore a bluish gray, tight-fitting uniform of rough cloth. Heather was aware of thinking that the fabric looked scratchy. She was searched and stripped, then given clothes and told to put them on; blue jeans, a blue tee shirt, and white thongs. Without moving, she stared at the clothes. The guard ordered her a second time to change into them, after which she was led into a room full of women. About half were black-skinned and the rest divided almost evenly between brown-skinned and white-skinned. They were all dressed the same as she.

When given the choice by the guard to go into the general company of the female jail population, or be locked into the cell she had been assigned, Heather answered barely above a whisper, "The cell, please." The big woman chuckled, led her through the room, pulled out keys from a retractable device on her belt and unlocked a cell door. Heather walked inside to the nearest bed, and sat down stiffly, her back to the room with its milling throng and unruly shouting. She heard the cell door shut with a loud metal clang, and the key turning in the lock. Instinctively, Heather felt this locking in was safe because it divided her from what all her fresh innocence told her was imminent danger in this unwieldy body of criminal women.

She didn't know how long she sat there, nor what she was seeing as she stared at the wall across from her. Time had stopped. If only she could catch time and ride it backwards to erase this horror.

But we belong to the flow of time. We are attached at a certain point created just for us since before the foundation of the world. We are its prisoner, but it lends and frees every life to its purpose.

Heather clutched the small clear plastic bag issued to her by the heavy lady with the chuckle like it was her last vestige of refuge. Never had she been more frightened. From out of this numb fear and agony, she heard a voice behind her, "What cha' in for?"

Turning slightly, Heather saw a middle-aged white woman on the other side of the bars. Timidly, she answered, "Passport violation."

"Sandy's my name," the woman offered, seemingly unimpressed with Heather's crime, "What's yours?"

"Heather."

"Hi, Heather." The woman sat down outside the cell and began painting her toenails. Heather smelled the strong scented fumes and thought of her own polishes back home sitting quietly atop the round mirror with its pounded pewter frame, pewter balls for legs, and beveled mirror with perfect scallops running around its edge. "Don't be shy," the woman said between bouts of holding her breath to polish the next toe. "Get to know the girls." Finished with the last toenail, she stood up, straining her toes apart, and waddled away on her heels, like a penguin.

Heather wished she could calm her pounding heart.

"Don't grab the damn phone!" An enormous black girl held the receiver of a wall phone in a club-like position, threatening a white girl.

"It's my turn!" the white girl screamed, her face flushed red as she grabbed for the receiver.

"Don't grab the damn phone!" the black girl yelled again, pushing her back.

Heather had no place to hide. She had no way to protect herself from this violent sight, from the many-headed monsters that creep in the night as the child screams in fear through an uncompassionate door, beyond which the family hears but does nothing.

"Calm down!"

"Shut up!"

"Stuff it!" were cries from others, now watchful of the mounting tension between the black and white girl.

Curling her lips outward, the white girl lunged again for the receiver, screaming hysterically, "It's my turn!"

A cold feeling spread through Heather's body. She felt as though she was on a sled slamming down a hill of ice with no way to stop.

The receiver was thrown by the black girl with such force it bounced between the end of its cord and the wall repeatedly, and fast, like a ricocheting bullet. Arms gathered around the black girl, like black and white ropes to keep her from attacking the white girl, who now stood red-faced, whimpering like a child, "It's my turn; it's my turn."

Heather heard the sound of keys, like heavy loose change in a pocket, followed by a guard yelling, "Lock up!" The stampede is over. The animals will be penned.

Cursing filled the air. Playing cards were thrown angrily onto table tops and personal items grabbed with swift power.

From this display, Heather realized the open area was the more popular one, and the disagreement between the black girl and the white girl had caused the privilege to be revoked from all. With dread, she watched to see who sifted out of the general movement toward her cell. Seven women were due, because there were eight beds. They were arranged by twos, as bunk beds, at each corner of the cell.

What if one was the black woman or the white woman she had just seen with their vulgar tempers? Mercifully, those two went elsewhere. Sandy was among the seven women who entered her cell and made introductions all around. Heather hadn't expected politeness in jail.

The guard walked along the bars. A key into a lock, a twist of the wrist, a metal screech, and the harsh realization of incarceration. A cell, 12 feet by 12 feet, and seven strange women of questionable valor.

An exposed toilet stood between the furthest bunks. Its public nature shredded the last shred of dignity.

For hours Heather sat motionless. Her's was an upper bunk nearest to the bars. She rested her head against the cold steel, her eyes sweeping again and again over the same Venetian-blind covered windows, the same walls, the same TV set on the counter in its placid 'off' position, the same mysterious pattern of lines painted on the floor three or four feet from the thick-glassed end of the room, through which she saw three female guards sitting atop desks in an office talking to one another. It was an empty desolate view. If she were deaf she might think, except for the three guards behind the glass and the seven women in her cell, the place was otherwise vacant. But she wasn't deaf, and what she heard were streams of abusive language, volleys of name-calling, and occasional verbal assault gone too far and reciprocated angrily until others coaxed it calm, and by these sounds she knew the unimaginable was real.

These noisy recesses of low human caste began screaming for dinner, not a footman ringing a delicate crystal bell to announce an artistic gourmet meal, but more the stamp of hungry cattle lowing for mash. Again the keys jingled, the guard turned the locks, and the doors slid open. Female bodies rushed, pushing one another to be first.

"Come on," Sandy said, walking past her, then "wait a minute." She turned and walked back to the metal box affixed to her bunk. Pulling out a white plastic fork, knife, and spoon, she handed them to Heather. "I have an extra set. Hang on to them, they don't issue these."

Heather stared at the three pieces encased in a see-through covering, stunned that they had been raised to the level of an important commodity in this jail society. What would be laughed at to be considered precious by the outside world, kept humanity here one notch above the beast.

A piece of white bread atop which sat a small square of butter; cracked green peas; a thick slice of canned turkey; brown gravy, the consistency of water; milk from a small carton; and a pastry that looked like a beginning baker's reject, represented dinner. Now Heather understood why she heard about prisoners going on strike for better food.

Heather judged, by the pieces of bread flying back and forth, that bread was in high demand. One piece could buy all the food on a tray. Desserts were skulked over and hidden away, or if eaten, its predator watched defensively between soggy bites. Even if the food had been appetizing, Heather knew she couldn't eat after watching the heavy woman across from her. The woman's face was barely three inches above her plate, and her fork, which she grabbed as though it were a handlebar, was employed in a full bombardment onto her food. She was using her mouth as the door to a storage bin and the race was how quickly all the food from the plate could be shoveled through the opening.

The woman looked up with mumpy, food-swollen cheeks. A trickle of brown gravy escaped the corner of her mouth as she stared at Heather, seemingly heedless of the dribble now run down her chin and splashed back into the plate. Heather felt a bump against her leg under the table and turned toward Sandy. It was only a flicker, but she saw it, Sandy's warning; so she quickly busied herself over her own plate again. She didn't look at the big woman anymore, but her ears couldn't shut out the sound, like little screams of help from the food, as the woman's massive mouth beat it to a squishy pulp.

Heather heard it stop suddenly; this sound of the woman's slurpy chewing, like paste pulling apart each time her mouth opened in readiness for the next crush. Then, like a loud sour trombone note, the woman issued forth a belch. Like a growl from deep caves it came. Sound, pinched into individual compartments, but chained together; brown sound; ruptured sound. A piece of smelly air from the issuance reached Heather's nostrils. She closed her eyes and tightened her teeth, careful lest the woman should notice her reaction of abhorrence.

After a few moments, Heather looked up as casual as possible. The woman was looking off, down the table at the others. Her finger glistened as the saliva from her mouth, where she was using her finger as a toothpick, drooled around it. The big woman removed her fat finger from her mouth with a sucking sound, then dried it on the front of her blue tee shirt. Heather saw the stains left behind on the cloth, then quickly employed herself at cutting the turkey on her plate, even knowing she had no intention of eating it.

The table, one of ten joined together end to end, jiggled as the woman pushed back and stood up. She stood a full minute, during which Heather didn't look up, afraid she might draw the woman's attention. The sound of a zipper reached her hearing. By keeping her head bent over her plate, but lifting her eyes, Heather could see as high as the huge woman's waist. She dared to raise her eyes, a vague comprehension of the purpose of the zipper sound settling within her. Then she saw it, a puffy hand reaching inside and scratching.

"Come on." It was Sandy.

Heather jumped from the table and followed Sandy to a large plastic garbage can where the food remaining on the trays was dumped before the trays were stacked onto a nearby cart. She saw food on the floor trailing between the garbage can and the cart, and red liquid from the dessert running down the sides of the can, as though from a head injury. "Wasn't that gross?" Sandy whispered.

"What?"

"That fat chick, did you see her scratch herself?"

"Yes, it was gross, and thanks for warning me back there."

"That's okay, kid, but you have to be careful in here. I can tell you don't got no experience and it can get nasty sometimes. The best thing to do is mind your own business. Most of these girls get in trouble because they try to mind somebody else's."

Heather wanted to ask why Sandy was here, but that would be minding someone else's business she realized, so she kept quiet.

"Want to play Hearts?"

"Hearts?"

"Come on, I'll teach you."

Heather followed Sandy to a table cleared now from the meal she couldn't convince her mind to call dinner. She tried to concentrate on card-playing, but her attention flew to the raucous talk and frequent flare-ups. Except for Sandy, she spoke only when spoken to, and was relieved when the time in the open area was over and eight women each went into their cells.

Chapter Fourteen

At 11 p.m. the lights were turned off, except for one dim bulb against the opposite wall. The verbal calling went on for a while, until overcome by shouts of "Pipe down!" "Go to sleep!" "Shut up!" and finally...finally it was still enough to examine the events that had brought her to this place.

Love was all of it, love for a man. She had promised devotion and obedience to Arthur in good times, and now in these horrific times. The descending stairway to this place was because she loved him. She would always love him, but she admitted being jailed was a result of her desperate illegal attempts to help Arthur.

Maybe Aunt Claire had been right. She heard this thought in her mind and was nearly overcome by it. Not once, until now, had she faltered to believe Arthur's cause was the highest priority. She had lost herself in it; her honesty, her dignity, her sense of right and wrong; all of it had been banished for Arthur's sake. "What about me?" came to the top for the first time.

Heather reflected on a girl she knew who married her high school sweetheart, had two children, and was satisfied to turn her back on whatever lay beyond the boundaries of her small hometown and her family-related activities. Heather, on the other hand, had wanted to reach out to the world, to embrace and heal it through a career in nursing. She had considered missionary work, perhaps going to India where she knew countless souls were afflicted and dying from want of even minimal care. Then Arthur, her prince of light, even with his extravagant ways, entered and surrounded her heart like an enclosure made to hold a spirited horse in preparation to break it to his bridle and saddle. Her freedom and vision were swept away like a butterfly taken by the wind, and he had become her essence and her meaning. Her existence was centered in him alone. She glanced at the chipped black wall phone, cold and still under the dim spotlight above it. That black box was a connection to Arthur, to the voice that could make sense in this danger and babble around her. But she dared not approach the machine; she dared not become vulnerable during free time out of their cells, to those pushing and stamping in line to dial their numbers in hopes of escaping this trap.

Squeezing her eyes shut and lowering her head until her chin rested against her chest, Heather knew this is where it all had led. She was caged, debased to the state of an animal locked in a human zoo. A pain, somewhere a deep ache that seemed to come from everywhere inside of her all at once, filled her senses. Sitting up taller, she leaned back against the cold cement wall as tears began streaming down her cheeks.

Everyone seemed asleep and she was careful in her movements lest she awaken someone. The east and the west were closer than this utter failure of her expectations for herself and her life. Never, could she have envisioned this. A felon! That's what she was by law because false passports were automatically a federal offense. There were no misdemeanors at the federal level; there were only degrees of felonies. She was a passport violator and therefore she was a felon. The thought weakened her.

When enough condemnation was spent upon herself, practical survival instincts took her away from this examination and self-recrimination. Difficult ideas and realities began tumbling into her thinking.

Arthur! He was planning on coming to pick up his passport tomorrow, after they had talked tonight, but she hadn't called him from the booth near the fire station as arranged. He would never imagine where she was! How wildly she hoped he wouldn't proceed with his intentions. Surely he would know something had gone wrong when he didn't hear from her. Surely he would! Don't let anything happen to Arthur, she prayed again and again in her soul. For the first time in Heather's life, she felt despair deep enough to want to die. This humiliation was more than she could endure.

Then something she learned many years earlier when Aunt Claire was helping her through an adolescent agony came back to her. The particular details of the incident escaped her, but the message rang clear and pure through the corridors of time. It was a warm syrupy memory, and spoke of how God never gave His children more in life than they could bear. Aunt Claire said God knows how weak humans are. "We can't even make a star," she would say. Heather almost heard her Aunt's voice saying it now, then adding how God allows troubles to strike, but always, she stressed, He gives an escape, a way out when the storm could no longer be borne. Okay, Heather decided, she wouldn't crack apart, she couldn't crack apart.

Tomorrow, first thing, she must get word to Arthur, and the telephone was the only link she had. A shudder ran through her at the thought of making herself vulnerable, but she had to call Arthur no matter what threat that meant to her safety. Perhaps there would be a time when no one was anxious to use the phone. She would watch, and then she would act.

His hideaway phone number was tattooed on her heart. Heather doubted even after Arthur no longer used that phone if she could ever forget those seven combined numbers that opened his voice to her.

She must have drifted into sleep because it was daylight when she opened her eyes to Sandy's shaking. "Come on, make your bed. The guard's coming down the line for a count. If you ain't ready you don't get no breakfast."

Heather wondered how she had slept through the tumult in her soul and the loud stirrings of a jail morning. Everyone was up and ready. "Hurry!" Sandy yelped.

The guard laughed at Heather's frantic last rush, then gave her a stern look and continued down the line. Later, looking at breakfast, Heather decided it would not have been a loss. Powdered eggs; the reliable piece of white bargaining bread flying from hand to hand; bitter lukewarm coffee; and an orange were the offerings. She ate the orange.

Heather kept her eye on the black wall phone. It represented an exit over this stake of fire. Again, the eating had been in the center of the rectangular room and tumultuous. Again, the manners were gross and animalistic. Again, the card playing and television dominated as recreation. Again, Heather knew she was threatened by the volatile natures of these women milling around her.

After scraping her plate into the can that oozed with food

down its outer length, she looked longingly toward the phone. It was the first time she would be away from Sandy's side. "Just walk over there and use it," Sandy said. "Don't look at anybody and if someone comes up and wants to use it, say 'good bye', hang up, and then come back here and sit beside me. Nothing will happen if you do it exactly that way." Some additional minutes had been required after Sandy's instructions before Heather could muster her courage. It felt as though she had to walk through a gauntlet of ready whips to reach her destination. Then sharply, she declared in her thinking, "I have to do this!" and in a flash was up and over to the phone, dialing Arthur's number.

He answered on the first ring. Heather was startled by the solid sound of her husband's voice. It connected her to outside life, and for a moment she couldn't speak because its comforting reality overwhelmed her.

Caution creeping into his tone, Arthur repeated, "Hello?"

"Arthur," Heather whispered.

"Turtle?"

"Yes, it's me."

"I've been trying all night to reach you. I drove by our house and when I saw the place was dark, I crept inside to check things out. I was afraid..." he hesitated "... that 'Georgie Boy' may have hurt you. You're okay, aren't you? Where are you? What's going on?"

"I'm in jail."

"What!"

"Yes, jail."

"What the hell for?"

"Passport violation."

There was a weighty pause, a nothingness of sound, like a road in a desolate valley that runs forever as a line into the distance then disappears at the horizon, all through a haze of profound silence.

"Arthur?"

"Yea, yea, I'm here," he answered softly. "Tell me about it."

Quickly she relived each step, ending with, "You can't pick up your passport or you'll be arrested too."

He answered in a voice barely above a whisper, "Okay."

Heather waited what seemed like forever for him to continue. Finally, he asked, "Have you called your Aunt?"

"No."

"Have you called an attorney?"

"No."

"I'll do both." Again there was an agonizing silence, long and disturbing to Heather. The green tunnel is red because you are alone within it, and have only your destiny to break free of its deadly force. "Are you sure you're all right, Turtle? I mean, no one there has hurt you or anything?"

"No. I've made a friend named Sandy. She's keeping me safe."

Another long silence came for answer but this time Heather couldn't wait for him to break it. "Arthur, what are we going to do?"

As though he hadn't heard her, he repeated, "Are you sure you're okay?"

"Yes, but what are we going to do?" she repeated.

"I'm going to call your Aunt Claire," he answered, "now get back to Sandy and don't leave her side."

"But Arthur..."

"No buts. Go!"

Heather felt worse after talking to Arthur than before she called. What had she expected, she asked herself. Did she believe Arthur could fix her predicament in a moment and free her from the talons surrounding her? Of course he couldn't, that would take time. But his eagerness to be off the phone disturbed her. She decided his urgency was because he was worried about her having an incident in the jail population and he was anxious to begin the process of releasing her. That was reason enough for haste. Yet, something in her deeper intuitive feminine nature felt wronged by his hurry to be off the phone. She didn't understand it; she only knew it was how she felt.

It was Saturday, during lock-up, between breakfast and lunch that the guard came. "Heather Conway?"

"Yes?"

"You have a visitor, come on," the guard ordered.

"How come you're so lucky?"

"Wish I had a damn visitor!"

"My old man is coming next week," were the reactions as she was led the length of the room along the outside of the locked cells. Growls, snarls, hisses, and foul language from the cells marked her passage and spoke of chilling depravity regarding these women.

Heather followed the guard through a series of metal doors, each closing heavily behind her. She exfoliated captivity and drew closer to the free blue sky with each slamming. The room into which she was led was small and cubicle. It measured approximately six feet by twelve feet. Four telephones sat in private-walled compartments on her side of a thick glass partition. The phones' counterparts sat on a shelf on the opposite side of the glass for the visitor's use.

The guard sat on a stool behind her and waited. Heather was certain it would be Arthur and she fought to control her need to see his face and to hear his reassurance about obtaining an attorney and about...movement caught her eye and she looked up.

Her aunt walked quickly to the phone and picked up the receiver. Heather sat on her side of the glass, not moving, as something inside of her tried to reconcile why Arthur hadn't come. Aunt Claire tapped the glass and pointed to the phone on Heather's side. Heather lifted the receiver to her ear.

"Are you all right?" Aunt Claire leaned closer to the glass and that small gesture felt like a swamping of love toward her. Tears streamed from Heather's torture, they poured down her face and splashed onto the counterpane. Her body trembled and she gasped, unable to speak for several minutes.

Aunt Claire put her hand on the glass at the level of the top of Heather's head and in that movement conveyed a sense of soothing her tattered spirit. "Shh, Shh," Aunt Claire coaxed through their telephone connection. "I have an attorney and we're getting bail."

"Bail?" Heather looked straight through the glass at her aunt's face. "How much do they want?"

"$15,000.00. That's 10% of the $150,000.00 they're asking."

"Aunt Claire! Where can you get that much cash?"

"Don't you worry about that," Aunt Claire responded, giving Heather a reassuring wink.

"Come on, Conway," the guard barked, "time's up; you wasted it blubbering."

Hurriedly, Aunt Claire finished, "I've put $50.00 on your books, and I promise you will be out of this place as soon as possible. Meanwhile, be careful?" Heather saw tears glisten in her aunt's eyes.

With each of the sealing doors behind her, she was taken down again through the levels of the nether world, where yellow eyes watched and tongues forked and icy hearts laid in wait. The air was dusty and water seeped through the rock walls.

"We get a movie this afternoon!" Sandy gushed, as the guard opened the cell for Heather to enter. Sandy made her feel safe in an environment Heather knew was full of trickery and danger. That afternoon, after lunch, the women gathered in the open area as a guard set up the film in the center of the room then left it running and went back to the office behind the glass partition at the end of the room. It was a cartoon about a pink panther. Heather sat on the outer back edge of the crowd, aware she couldn't separate herself completely without drawing attention to herself. Yet she couldn't enter this society because it was a wild fire she didn't know how to quell, so she sat, not out and not in. Sandy had opted to sit in the front row and told Heather to come up to her if any problem developed. Find me, find me quickly.

With the shouting, both at the film story and each other, Heather wasn't able to hear the movie's dialogue. Then suddenly, all the women fell silent, too silent, she thought. She heard it, the smuggled sound of bodies moving quickly, quietly. A circle of women had formed, surrounding some action. In a moment, Heather realized whatever mischief was taking place was condoned, since the women who stood in a circle watching, cast glances towards the guards' station as a look-out would.

General exclamations, as of awe, issued from the clustering women. Heather saw an enormous black woman lift a white woman with a bloodied face by the hair, then smash the white woman's face against the bars. Heather wanted to vomit. Why didn't the other women stop it? Why weren't they sickened by this?

Are you alive, or are you dead with maggots in your hearts?

The struggling pair fell to the floor again, but a movement in the crowd caused a gap through which Heather could see. The white girl was flat on her back, less than half the size of the black girl who sat straddling her, and now, in addition to bloodying her face, reached up under the white girl's jail blue tee-shirt and grabbed her bare breasts. No one interfered. The black girl kept on, and Heather looked away, feeling bloodied by what she saw. The guards! Where were the guards?

Grunting, the black woman raised her immense body to a standing position. Slowly, the white girl stirred and raised herself to her feet also. Heather couldn't hear what it was the white girl said, but the black girl's answer was loud, "You ain't never gonna be black, not even with that frizzy hair!" She grabbed the white girl by the hair and smashed her bleeding face into the bars again.

There was general yelling now, which brought the guards, and whose appearance dissolved both the fight and the crowd. "Lock up!"

The typical reactions ensued. "Shit!" "Damn!" "Hell!" and worse as the women headed for their cells. Heather heard someone say the black and white girl involved in the dispute were taken to "solitary", but she didn't ask more about what that meant. She was glad they were gone and wished the memory of what they left behind could have gone with them.

For the remainder of the day, especially at dinner when the women mingled, Heather hung close to Sandy, not daring to look anyone in the eyes, not daring to risk opening herself to the wrong person. Later, back in their cell playing cards, Sandy asked, "You got kids?"

"No, do you?"

"Yea. I got four kids."

"Four! Boys or girls?"

"Three girls and one boy. My oldest is like me. I never see her on account of it. I've been nine years in the joint and I ain't seen her once."

"That's sad."

"No it ain't. I won't see her because I don't want her to take after me. Figure it won't happen if she don't have nothin to see and pattern after."

"Do you see your other children?"

165

Tears started in Sandy's eyes.

"I'm sorry," Heather apologized, "I didn't mean to pry."

"You ain't prying," Sandy answered, before blowing her nose, "just makes me remember." She leaned toward Heather, lowering her voice to a whisper. "I took the rap for my boy. He was only 21. I figured I knowed this game better and could handle it."

"You mean you..."

"Yea, but that's between me and you."

"What did he..."

"Heroin. He was dealing," Sandy answered, her eyes glistening with tears again. "At first he was real good. He sent letters and money and came to visit. But it started tapering off, you know, little by little, until poof, it was gone."

"How long has it been since you've seen him?"

"More than two years. He's forgot his Mama. Too busy out there to remember me rotting in jail for him."

"Have you written to him?"

"Nah. Never was much good at writing. Gets me though. He knows how hard it is in here." Sandy's voice thickened. She put her cards down and slipped off Heather's bed, walking to her own lower bunk then leaned against the wall, staring off.

Heather wasn't sure how to react to Sandy in this setting, so she sat a long while in uncertainty and puzzlement. Her hesitancy was interrupted when commissary order blanks were handed through the bars to each girl. Now Heather understood what Aunt Claire had meant when she said she put $50.00, the maximum amount allowed at a time, on her books.

Still feeling sorry for Sandy, Heather eased over the edge of the bunk and walked to the end of Sandy's bunk. She remembered, earlier, Sandy running her hand through her hair and commenting how nice it would be to wash her hair with shampoo instead of soap. "Sandy?"

Sandy turned and looked at her with dull eyes, full of damage.

"I'm sorry," Heather said, sitting down gently. The gesture seemed somehow to embrace Sandy without touching her.

"That's okay, kid, you didn't mean no harm."

"Hey, I'm flush," Heather chirped.

"You got female trouble?"

Heather blushed. "No, I mean I have $50.00 on my books and I thought you might help me spend it."

Sandy stared hard into Heather's eyes, then softly answered, "That's the nicest thing I've heard in a long time."

They bent over the commissary list together. "How about shampoo?" Heather suggested.

"Tough!" Sandy answered.

"Candy bars?"

"Tough!" Sandy's smile widened.

"Tooth paste?"

With authority, Sandy concluded, "You don't want to waste your money!"

"Doughnuts?"

"Tough."

"Apples?"

"Nah!"

"Pencils?"

Sandy snapped her attention onto Heather. Her eyebrows raised, causing fleshy waves on her forehead. "Pencils! Now what the hell would I do with pencils?"

Heather wasn't able to conceal a smile. "Sorry," she offered.

Sandy shifted her attention back onto the list, rubbing her hands together as though over a fire on a cold winter night.

Heather read each item for Sandy's approval or disapproval, and felt as though she was on a shopping spree; twirling in a black sequined dress, and trying on dozens of silk gowns. Should she take the green silk or the pink? The apple or the chocolate bar? They were women out shopping and it didn't matter if it was diamonds or shampoo, there was money to spend and that alone was glorious.

When they finished, Sandy added the sum of their choices. "Holy cow! $90.00! Come on, kid, we got some serious weeding to do!"

They debated, considered and weighed one thing against another until the surplus was eliminated and those things wanted and needed most remained. For nearly two hours they had been at their task. Heather let out a gush of air and flopped back on Sandy's bunk. "I feel like I've been working all day." She rolled her head in Sandy's direction. "What time does our order come tomorrow?"

"After noon sometime. I can taste those doughnuts already!"

"I think I'll do a little writing," Heather said, raising herself.

"Sure, Kid. Thanks. You're okay."

"It was fun," Heather answered, then climbed back onto her bunk feeling glad that Sandy was in good spirits again.

A dozen times she started a letter to Arthur, but her mind wouldn't focus long enough to write a complete thought. This jail life around her was too explosive for concentration. It was too slicing in white hot wire through her entrails.

"Do you roll cigarettes?"

"Beg your pardon?"

It was the girl in the bunk beneath her. "Cigarettes? Do you roll em?"

"I don't smoke."

"Wanna learn?"

Heather hesitated at the offer, then thought it best to agree. "Sure."

The girl handed up a fat pouch of tobacco then climbed onto Heather's bunk. She was white, tall, and thin, with two greasy strands of hair that fell forward on each side of her face, partially concealing the bright pink acne mingled with old scars from former breakouts. Leaning sideways against the bars, she yelled, "Hey, Candy! Send some papers to C!"

The cry was taken up along the line to Candy, somewhere at the other end of the room, who yelled back, "You owe me a tattoo, Angel!"

"Okay! Okay!" Angel screamed, "Send the papers!"

Hoots, whistles and curses marked the passage of the rolling papers. Finally, an arm protruded into sight from the next cell with the papers held between white fingers. Angel took the papers. "Thanks, Candy!" she hollered.

"You owe me a tattoo!"

"Yea, all right!" Angel returned.

"What does she mean?" Heather figured the question was safe.

"Oh, nothing," Angel answered, "They think I draw good so I draw pictures on their envelopes to the outside, that's all. I get little things for it, you know, give and take."

It never occurred to Heather there was talent among these women. She had already learned through listening why some of them were here; murder, drug trafficking, postal embezzlement, armed robbery; words and ideas that away from Hollywood movie screens were factually and humanly embodied in these living breathing females around her. Some looked abnormal, either in their innate arrangement of face and body, or in the way they acted. But most of the women looked like any woman in the grocery store buying groceries for her family.

"May I see the next envelope you draw?"

"Sure. Why not? Look here. This is how you roll."

Angel laid the paper between the underside of the index and middle finger of her right hand and reached with her left for the tobacco. At once, Heather knew Angel was left-handed. "You fill it with tobacco." Angel's eyes didn't leave the work at her fingers. She let the tobacco fall as though she was carefully regulating the fall of precious saffron spice. "See how I use my thumbs?" She used both thumbs and index fingers to roll the mixture into a tight cigarette. "And the jam." She ran her tongue along the gummed edge to seal the paper, then held the homespun cigarette up by its end. "Here, take a look."

Heather took the cigarette and looked it over. It was tightly packed and even in diameter from tip to tip.

"That's your sample," Angel said, "Now roll. I gotta do that envelope."

The first attempts wouldn't stay together and bulged in the center. But after ten or twelve tries, the cigarettes became more even along their length, although they weren't as tight as Angel's. Heather became immersed in the challenge and before long cigarettes lay across her bed like a row of white bullets.

"Lights out!"

Heather was surprised by the guard's call. Time had raced this evening. She gave the cigarettes to Angel and genuinely exclaimed over the roses and vines emerging on the envelope in red and blue inks.

Chapter Fifteen

Heather called Arthur once more, but he was adamant that she not call again, saying she was in danger to be on the phone with him and he wouldn't allow it. As soon as was humanly possible he would have her freed. Reluctantly, she acquiesced. She gave in because her heart was afraid and trusting.

Another day passed without changes in her jail society. This particular night, Sunday, was the first evening that had quiet to it. Each woman seemed to be involved in a personal project. Sandy had played game after game of Solitaire. Another was writing to her husband who she called her "old man." Earlier, Heather had heard that same girl telling a cellmate how jail time is easier when you have a husband and children waiting for you on the outside. She was a dark pretty girl, of Mexican descent, and she was intelligent. From general conversations within the cell, Heather realized this girl had been a postal employee and figured out a way to intercept social security checks. The girl had usurped their passage and taken the money for herself. No one is watching, save One.

Heather learned that this jail was a halfway place for these women. All of them were prison inmates being transferred from one prison to another. No one mentioned what prison they had just left, or to what prison they were going. She wondered how this in-between jail place was, compared to an actual prison.

Heather was repeatedly shocked by the bragging of illegal, immoral, horrid deeds these women had perpetrated and how they seemed not to care, feel sorrow, or regret. There was no "I'm sorry" for what may have been a harmful or deadly result to others that flowed from their atrocious acts. Many of them discussed new cunnings and shared methods of shoplifting and robbery. It was a college of sorts, where the pupils were given A's for the worst truancy; where violence was glorified and envied; where the worst was the best, and the best was the worst; where wisdom was foolishness, and foolishness was wisdom.

How sorrowful it must make the Creator to watch these souls open to the devil's rule and his never-ending hellish attacks.

Where did these ways begin? How did they grow? Heather knew these were not children with foolish hearts, but grown women with foolish hearts. Why didn't she hear intentions to turn from their destructive paths and become renewed and join into life with a cleansed and decent participation? Why didn't they desist from the self-inflicted damage? Why did she only hear new plans, new traps, and eagerness to be free in order to strike again in more clever ways? She couldn't understand why this incarceration experience didn't make immediate saints out of these women.

The human heart lies hidden, and the closest we come to knowing it is by the measure of another's behavior, not by the words they offer. We are taught: By its fruit we shall know the tree. Know the fruit, and you will know the tree.

Somehow, in spite of an engrossed and detailed conversation the two women across from her bunk were having about how to steal designer clothes from department stores, the evening was almost peaceful. The entire line of cells had been quiet, except for occasional bursts of obnoxious language. She wondered if a quiet magnetic moon was rising into the sky and having its influence on earth below. Perhaps the moon was a silver Crescent with one bright star in its empty belly and these jewels were alone in the clear sky not yet dark enough for the pollen-strewn night.

Or the full moon! Heather thought, as the lights went out with a sudden snap. Heather thought how the moon was shining above Aunt Claire's house, above Arthur in his hideaway motel, above their home and the crystal hanging in her kitchen window, perhaps this very moment breaking moonlight into pieces of light and fluttering it like illumined fairies throughout the room she knew so well. She imagined the moon gaining prominence over the stars by playing spotlight; its light a dainty curtsy as it crossed the stage of night. And behind the lighted orb, a dark curtain with tiny specks of light, masses of universal fire, marking other possible existences, and all of that compared to this belittled cell.

Her sleep was fraught with nightmares. Faces of women,

close up, screeched from behind bars. Their hands gripped and shook the iron fence. Arms reached out trying to grab her. Tears ran down faces that melted into leather-like skin over the skulls. Eyes were vacant from their sockets. There were no teeth, and mouths moved without sound. Fingers turned bony and made a cracking sound as they reached for her.

And one hand touched her. Its cold deathlike fingers wrapped around her throat and pulled her near so other hands could grab her. She felt the hard bones against her. She heard the sound of howling-wind through the empty ribs, echoing the miseries of humanity. She was pulled into a cell, surrounded and forced to the ground. Above her they stood, a circle of grotesque faces. They bent down, their death faces coming nearer and nearer.

Heather awoke to find her heart pounding wildly. She was hot and perspiring. Sitting up, she stared into the darkness. There were no voices, only snoring, occasional dream mumbles, and the squeak of springs from bodies turning in their sleep. A sick feeling filled her and a cold chill of flesh bumps passed over her body.

She turned outward, her face against the bars, and stared hard at nothing. Then once again, she was pulled by the powerful need for sleep. The next thing she knew it was early the following morning. Stretching somewhat awake, she heard whisperings from the next cell, then the word, "Heather", and "pull a train." To hear her name issue from a neighboring cell surprised her, but she made nothing more of it, resolving to ask Sandy when the jail population arose for the new day. For another hour or so, her sleep was broken and fitful until she realized her cellmates were stirring, and she awakened. After making the bed and arranging her personal hygiene as best she could under these captive conditions, Heather went over to Sandy and asked quietly, "Sandy, what does 'pull a train' mean?"

Without looking up and without so much as a flutter of concern or interest, Sandy answered, "It means a gang rape."

"Dear God! Precious Lord in Heaven! Sweet Jesus!" Heather returned to her bunk and climbed upon it. Her body felt numb, her mind was a jumble, and her soul churned. Mental horror was so strongly upon her, at first she didn't realize her name was

172

being called repeatedly from outside the cell. After Sandy called her name sharply, Heather turned towards the summons.

A guard was at her cell door urging her to hurry. Her bail had been paid in full. "Christmas Morning! The Light of the World! Amen!"

She had enough presence of mind to wish a good-bye and thank-you to Sandy, who didn't try to hide her sadness that Heather was leaving.

Heather was led through the door separating the inmates from the guards' station and told to wait while the guard stepped inside the office for paperwork. From here, she could look through the office door opening and over the desk tops to the window of thick glass through which the guards kept their unending vigil of the women prisoners on the other side of the pane.

The feel of her clothes was delicious and Heather stroked them in a tender loving way. They made her realize how completely she had been severed from normal life.

For these moments, she felt the way some soldiers do when they return home from a foreign war. After coming down a gangplank or an aircraft staircase, their first gesture is to get on their hands and knees and kiss the earth of home, even before they kiss their wife and children and parents and friends. She felt that way now, as though she were returned from a war, one which had nearly caused her mental and emotional life to bleed out.

There were two detectives in the hallway. They promptly handcuffed her and she was taken to a courtroom on another floor of that same building. She knew her bright red hair didn't help keep her from public attention along the way. Inevitably, the eyes of the person would glance at her hair, then her face, then her handcuffs, then at her face again. She wasn't helping the love of redheads, she mused.

The court arraignment was brief. All she understood was that she was being released on bail and was required to keep in communication and appear for a court date that would be set after a series of paperwork requirements. At last, she was led back to the place where she had originally entered this sick inner world. Here, the freshly arrested were booked in, and those newly released were booked out.

Heather sat quietly along a wall-bench while the two detectives completed her papers and retrieved her purse. Then the three of them entered an elevator. While it descended, one detective inserted a key into the lock of her handcuffs and she felt those shackles removed. It was another layer of suffocation from which she was delivered, and closer to breathing the sweet air of freedom.

They handed over her purse just as the elevator door opened. Aunt Claire was standing there. Heather rushed into her open arms and wasn't aware for several moments that the elevator door had closed and taken the two detectives back to the devil's haunt she knew would never be forgotten.

"Aunt Claire! How did you do it? $15,000.00!"

"Rose loaned me the money. She knows I'm good for it. I was stuck because of the weekend. It would have taken another day to liquidate a bond and have access to Heather looked past her aunt. "Where is Arthur? Isn't he with you?"

When Claire didn't answer, Heather shifted her attention from searching the lobby, back onto her Aunt's face. "What is it, Aunt Claire? Please tell me."

Claire took a deep breath. "I don't know where he is, Heather. He called me just after he heard from you and said he'd get back to me soon, but I haven't heard from him since."

"Aunt Claire! That was three days ago!"

That was four thousand years ago. Civilizations have sprung up and died since then. Arthur doesn't belong to history! Arthur belongs to me! Here! Now!

"I know," Claire softly answered. "I've driven by your house all times of the day and night. I've called your home number repeatedly and left messages. I even went to the door and knocked, but there has been no word from Arthur."

Incredulously, Heather stared at her aunt. For several moments their eyes met but no words were spoken. Too many possibilities were flying through Heather's thoughts to be slowed down by verbalizing each of them. One, however, dominated, and that was concern for Arthur's safety. "Aunt Claire, I'm going to tell you everything to the last detail. You will forgive me for all of it, I know you will, but I must call Arthur this moment." Wildly, Heather looked around the room and saw a set of phone booths recessed into a wall. She borrowed coins from her aunt then walked as fast as she could to the telephones. At the nearest booth, she hurried a coin into the slot then punched the seven memorized numbers that always led her to Arthur's voice. He was more than half of her heart and he was the only person that could make her's whole. The ringing of the phone on Arthur's end was forever, it was the Cheops pyramid, grain by grain, crumbling back into the orange Sahara.

Unable to accept this silence, she waited with an uncanny patience. She refused to believe that Arthur was not answering. Finally, she felt Claire's hand on her shoulder. "Come on, Heather, we'll go to your house. Maybe he's left a note there for you."

"Yes, of course, he'll have some message for me there," Heather answered hopefully. "For a moment I was worried."

During the drive Heather shared her plight, and the jail life experience with its intense dangers. Her aunt only looked disturbed once, when Heather talked about searching the "Little Angels" section of the cemetery for her's and Arthur's aliases.

When she finished, Claire reached over and squeezed her niece's hand. "You're safe now."

"Yes, and never will I do anything to grace the inside of a jail cell again." Hesitating, then adding quietly, she attested, "Not even for love."

They pulled up in front of Heather's house and both entered the dwelling.

It was quiet as an empty well, and oddly cold. Heather moved silently into the bedroom, not certain why she chose that direction other than that she was obeying some inner instinct. She scanned the large room, and at first saw nothing out of order, but little by little, she focused on the private parts of her and Arthur's life together. She approached his tall ebony-wood dresser. There she found the first signs to answer her questions; the first pieces of glass that slashed her softness. Arthur's undergarments were partially gone; socks, tee shirts, shorts. Atop the dresser his ivory cufflink container was missing. Next, she moved to the large walk-in closet, where 'his' and 'hers' wardrobes were kept on opposite sides, each enclosed behind sliding beveled-mirrored doors. She opened Arthur's and saw there had been activity there, and it was hasty because some shirts were hanging crooked from their wooden hangers and several pants had been tossed to the floor, in a rejected manner. Heather saw empty hangers. She even knew which certain favorite shirts of Arthur's these empty hangers represented. She glanced at the other end of his closet where boxes of expensive Italian shoes were stored in oak rectangles reaching from floor to ceiling. Here, also, was disarray. Some openings were empty. Again, Heather visualized the particular missing shoes, especially the delicately tooled leather boots and the hand-made Italian leather loafers. Gone. They were gone.

She felt it growing inside her, a part of her thinking was blank and another part was running panicked. She hurried to the bath vanity. Drawers stood open. Only items for a man's traveling were missing. Arthur's electric shaver, and sterling silver comb and brush set had vanished. Nothing on her side had been touched.

Why didn't words speak truth at this time? Why did she keep on, pounding the obvious like a stake through her heart? Then her pace slowed as though to brake the unwieldy speeding of her emotions. She re-entered the kitchen area where her aunt Claire stood quietly alongside the rosewood breakfast table. The many-spiked orchids there blossomed in peach and purple. Heather saw her aunt point to the tabletop.

Heather didn't understand. Slowly she approached, reluctantly focusing on the spot. It was small upon the table, and at first Heather didn't see it. That, and her wild state of mind refused the sight. Then it hit her awareness like a club. A circle of platinum, a band of promise, love exemplified, everything Heather had lived and breathed for lay in waste; symbolized by Arthur's discarded wedding ring. It wasn't tossed carelessly to land in some mangled fashion. It had been thoughtfully and deliberately placed exactly in a spot where it would suggest and tell all. As she crumbled, all she remembered were Aunt Claire's arms reaching around her.

Seven years passed. Heather was investigated those many years ago and found to be an absolute exception to what the courts anticipated. They had expected a drug trafficker, and instead found a good young woman who had committed a misstep; who had for the love of her husband veered a wrong way. She was set free, put on probation for three years, and required to check in with a probation officer once a month during that time. She was also conscripted to do forty hours of community time and those were spent working at a local hospital in the pediatrics department. For Heather, they were happy hours.

She moved to a small apartment and never heard from Georgie Boy.

Nursing school was her healing. She became a pediatric nurse. In fact, she was promoted to head nurse of pediatrics at Walnut Glen Hospital.

She stopped looking for Arthur, and waiting for Arthur, and longing for Arthur. Each time the phone rang she no longer rushed to it hoping it would be him.

The statute of limitation came to an end. Her husband had been missing for over seven years and she was no longer legally married.

Heather knew that never again would she sink to commit dishonest acts for anyone or anything. She also knew her love for Arthur was as strong as ever, but the awful long nights of agony and missing him were gone, finally.

In their place she had the babies and children at the hospital to love.

There was, however, a gold chain Arthur left behind. It was her gift to him in celebration of their first anniversary. He never took it off except once, to leave it behind when he disappeared.

Heather always wore the chain around her neck, and under her garments, out of sight. It had one ornament hanging from it; a platinum wedding band with the original inscription inside that read..."Forever."

The End